CW00410225

Kath Middleton began (100 words stories) and author Jonathan Hill's sec... has also contributed several of her short stories... anthologies. Her first solo work, *Ravenfold*, was published to much acclaim. Kath likes to put her characters in difficult situations and watch them work their way out. She believes in the indomitable nature of the human spirit (and chickens).

Praise for *Message in a Bottle*

"After reading other work by this author, I expected a dark twist, but instead it is very heart-warming. She portrays the confusion of grief and bereavement beautifully, as well as the intricacies of friendship of different kinds..." - *Lexie Conyngham, Author*

"Very good read indeed... It is a story about the value of friendship, understanding and forgiveness..." - *Elaine Gall, Amazon Top 50 reviewer*

"The story grasps from the outset as it explores love and friendships both old and new. Liz's life is suddenly struck by tragedy and as she struggles to come to terms with this she is challenged to question exactly what love means..." - *Harasrrek, Amazon reviewer*

First published in 2014 by Hilltop Press

ISBN-10: 1500495581
ISBN-13: 978-1500495589

Also by Kath Middleton:

Beyond 100 Drabbles (with Jonathan Hill)
Ravenfold

www.kathmiddletonbooks.com
www.facebook.com/ignite.bookblog
www.twitter.com/kathmidd

Message in a Bottle

Kath Middleton

For Michael.
Lovely to meet you.
Kath
x .

For Jonathan Hill

1

Liz was in the kitchen baking and singing along to some daft ditty on the radio when the knock came. She usually baked on a Saturday for a Sunday teatime treat. She enjoyed having the house to herself as it gave her the chance to get stuck in and make a mess. Gareth went out after lunch most Saturdays to meet his best friend, Miles; sometimes to go to the football, but often just to visit a pub for a drink or two, winding down after a hectic week at work.

Liz and Gareth had met at university and married as soon as they'd graduated. Liz was a top flight Fine Arts student whereas Gareth studied Physics. They say opposites attract and the arts and sciences met with a bang when the two of them got together. Miles had shared a flat with Gareth in their first year. He had graduated in business studies and the two men had ended up working for the same big engineering company. They had always got on well at university and still spent a lot of time together. Male bonding, she supposed you'd call it.

That afternoon it was a coffee and walnut cake,

Gareth's favourite. It amused her that he was such a baby for sweet stuff. She'd had the mixer running, beating air into the mixture to lighten it. She had gently folded in the flour and espresso coffee powder, then scraped it all out into a cake tin. She'd put the tin in the oven and had started to wipe up spilled flour from the worktop and put eggshells into the crock for recycling. The knock was loud. Peremptory. It echoed along the hall passageway and fell flatly through the open door of the kitchen.

Pushing back her hair, Liz wiped eggy hands down her floral apron and made her way down the hall to open the front door. She could see two looming shapes against the frosted glass of the leaded lights. As she pulled the door wide into the hallway, she stopped and stared at the police constables, a man and a woman, on her doorstep.

"Mrs Ellis?" the taller of the two queried.

"Yes," she said, unnerved by their sudden presence in her life.

"This is PC Thomas and I'm PC Wilder. Do you mind if we come in?" asked the other. She was smaller; only a girl really.

Liz went cold. This wasn't normal for a Saturday afternoon.

"Yes, of course. What is it? What's the matter? Is it Gareth?" She knew she was gabbling but she suddenly felt nervous. Shaky. Scared. She led them into the sitting room and indicated the chairs and sofa. "Please, sit down. Tell me what's wrong."

PC Wilder glanced at her colleague. It seemed that neither wanted to be the one to speak. The girl cleared her throat and began.

"I'm afraid it's your husband, Mrs Ellis. His car was involved in an accident. I'm sorry to have to tell you this but… he didn't make it. Sorry."

Liz just sat there, shocked into silence. She screwed her eyes tightly shut. She didn't want to see the police constables. She didn't want to have heard what they just said. She felt chilled and so, so heavy. Her whole body revolted and she thought she'd faint but no – that was a release offered to storybook characters. In real life, you bit your lip and got on with it.

"How? What happened? He was out with his friend. Was he there? Was Miles hurt?"

"I'm sorry, Mrs Ellis. There was no other person involved. The vehicle crashed into a tree. There will be a post-mortem of course - to see if we can find a reason. If your husband was taken ill suddenly or if there was any other factor."

"Any other factor?" Liz wasn't able to process information at the moment. Words assaulted her ears and she couldn't, didn't want to, make sense of them.

"We'll have to check for alcohol or drugs," the young PC explained gently.

"Yes, yes of course," Liz replied but she didn't

understand. Where had he been? Where was Miles?

Just then her telephone rang.

"Would you like me to stay with you?" PC Wilder offered. "Or can I contact someone to come and keep you company?"

"Oh, err... I don't know... Can I just see who this is?"

The phone was still ringing on the hall table.

"Hello? Oh, Miles! Oh God! Where are you? What's happening?" At this point Liz finally took in the fact that Miles, wherever he was, was alive, and Gareth was dead. She collapsed into huge, body-wracking sobs and the officer took the phone from her and spoke to Miles, while his colleague led Liz back to the chair and went into the kitchen to make tea.

Liz sat in an unlovely heap, wringing a wet tissue in her hands and hitching her chest with each sob. The male officer established that Gareth had never reached Miles' flat and had apparently hit the tree on the way there. She heard him tell Miles what had happened and could tell from the lack of response that Miles himself was stunned into silence for the moment. Liz took the proffered mug of steaming tea from the girl while her colleague continued to speak to Miles on the telephone.

"Mr Jeffries says he'll come round straight away, Mrs Ellis," the officer called from the hallway.

"Liz, please. Call me Liz."

"Very well, Liz. Would you like him to call here?"

"Oh, yes, please," she almost hiccupped between sobs. "I need to talk to him. He's, he was, my husband's best friend."

The female officer, who asked Liz to call her Ali, stayed with Liz until Miles arrived. When the doorbell rang, Ali let him in. Liz looked at him in total misery at first, then jumped up and ran to him. Miles had red eyes too and they stood hugging, comforting each other. It made Liz break out into fresh wails.

"If you're sure you'll be okay now, I'll go and join my colleague," Ali said. "And if you need any information, just give the local station a ring. I've left the contact details and a log number by your phone."

Liz broke away from Miles, gave a huge, horrible sniff and thanked Ali. "I'll let myself out," the girl said and with both officers out of the house, Liz collapsed onto the sofa.

"Miles! What do you think happened? I thought he was with you?" Just then there was a beeping from the kitchen and she leapt up to take the now meaningless cake from the oven. Working on automatic, she turned it out from the tin and put it on the cooling rack. She would probably give it to the birds. Cake now seemed so far away from the broken reality of her world.

"I don't know, Liz. He was on his way, obviously, but when he didn't arrive I began to wonder if he'd changed his mind. That's why I rang here. God, this is awful! What will we do without him?"

Miles looked over at her, his own face bleak. She remembered that he had known Gareth longer than she had.

"I can't take it in, Miles. I keep thinking someone will tell me this is all a joke – that it didn't happen. Or that it did and it was someone else. Mistaken identity. When I think back to earlier this morning, everything was fine. I had a lovely relaxing day ahead. I just feel now that it was all so trivial. I loved making things for Sunday tea. Now I feel like I'll never bake another cake in my life because I'll think about that knock on the door..." Her shoulders hunched again and she broke out into fresh sobs.

"Would you like me to stay tonight, Liz? You can't be alone – and to be perfectly honest I don't want to spend the evening left with my own thoughts either. Or would you rather I rang your mum?"

"No, for God's sake don't do that," she said with a sniffle. "She'll smother me. Yes, have the guest room. I just don't want to be alone and having someone who knew him as well as you did - well, you know what I've lost. You've lost him too."

They sat together talking quietly. It was a case of

"Do you remember how he used to…?" or, "Were you there that time when he…?" Liz found that talking about him hurt but not as much as trying to keep it all inside. They shared talk about Gareth and the times they'd spent with him, individually and together, as the evening drew on.

Eventually, shivering with shock, Liz tried to make some sandwiches.

"Give me that knife. You'll have your hand off!" Miles took the knife and cut the bread. "What have you got for sandwiches?" Liz couldn't rake her thoughts into a sensible heap so, while she was puzzling and frowning, he simply trawled through the fridge. They ate food that could have been sawdust and cotton wool, and finished up with a hot drink and some of the un-iced cake. It was unsatisfactory, but at that moment, they would have found no flavour in a banquet.

Approaching two in the morning they were both flagging, exhausted, but they knew they wouldn't sleep. Liz brought out some of Gareth's whisky. She wasn't a great drinker herself but knew he and Miles had often enjoyed a glass or two together.

"Let's drink a toast to him," she said, hot tears springing afresh as she swallowed hard.

"To Gareth. The best friend I ever had." Miles raised his glass.

"Gareth. A brilliant husband." Liz's voice broke on the last word.

They didn't go to bed as things turned out. Neither wanted to lie alone and think. They drank another stiff whisky and as the talk became more disjointed and the tears began to dry on Liz's cheeks, they slept where they sat, she on the sofa, he slumped in the armchair.

A dirty dawn light crept in and disturbed the inelegant pair as they snored and lolled in their seats. Liz was smacked in the face again by the awful truth as she clawed her way back to consciousness. She saw that Miles was stirring too and noticed the realisation of Gareth's death chasing away the traces of bemused wakefulness across his face.

"Hell! It's true isn't it? Yesterday really happened?"

"I wish it weren't but yes," he agreed. "I'll ring that policewoman shall I? See if we can find anything out. When the... when he'll be released for burial."

***

Over the next couple of days, the news that came through stunned Liz. Gareth had well over the legal limit of alcohol in his bloodstream.

"But he hadn't got to your place yet," she told Miles on the phone. "He hadn't had a drink at home, I'd swear it!"

"He must have stopped and bought it on the

8

way. But why? We were going to go out later to the match. He never drinks when he's at mine because he has to drive back."

The police told Liz they'd found the remains of a whisky bottle in the foot well on the driver's side of his car. It was impossible, owing to the condition of the vehicle, to tell how much had been left in it. Not much if his blood alcohol level was any guide. She found it so hard to take this in.

"Do you think he had any worries, Miles?" she asked next time he called round. "He seemed a bit preoccupied recently but then he often did. Just for a few days. As if he had some knotty problem to sort. He would always say it was work if I asked."

Miles looked thoughtful, puzzled, then doubtful.

"I couldn't say really, Liz. You know Gareth." He screwed his eyes up and winced for a second. He kept doing it. She did too, she knew. They kept using the present tense for a man they had to accept was in their past now. "He kept things inside. We might never know. Still, you know the worst now. You can make arrangements for his funeral."

"Oh Miles, I never thought I'd be doing this. Not for years! I don't know how I'll get through it."

"Come on. You'll cope. You're strong."

"But when people get older they talk about what they want when they're dead. You know, buried or cremated. Church or humanist - all that. I haven't a clue! We never got round to discussing it. It just

9

seemed so... distant, I suppose. Now... it's too late." She folded up again, tears falling afresh. It was too late for so much. Travelling the world; having children; retiring together.

2

A week later, Liz set out from the house to the crematorium. Her parents arrived there a little after she did. Her mother had come round to the house soon after she'd heard about the accident but Liz had got Miles to fend her off by giving her jobs. He had set her the task of organising a buffet at a local pub after the ceremony. It had kept her mum occupied and allowed her to feel she was helping.

Liz couldn't bear the thought of being the object of people's sympathy and feared that it made her seem aloof. The chapel was full of Gareth's university and work friends, Liz's friends, but only a cousin representing Gareth's own family. His parents were both dead - ironically in a car accident just before he went up to university. She and Miles together had chosen readings and pieces of music – no hymns. Gareth wasn't religious and it seemed important that they be true to him this one last time. The crematorium chapel was light and airy; tasteful pale oak furniture and wooden flooring had a calming effect.

She went through the ceremony in a daze, biting

her lips to prevent herself from breaking down. The awful moment when the coffin moved slowly towards the curtain to be cut off from sight almost broke her. Her mum didn't make it any easier by putting her arm round Liz at that very moment and trying to stroke her shoulder.

She forced herself to keep saying, "Thank you," trying to smile as people left the chapel and again during the buffet lunch as they approached to offer her their sympathies. She had no idea what she ate. Automatically she reached for a sandwich to give her hands something to do; to have somewhere to look other than into the eyes of others. She found she was thinking unworthy thoughts. Were they really sympathising with her or were they taking comfort from the fact that it had happened to her, not to them?

Miles came up to her as the number of bodies in the room thinned out.

"Are you going home after this?"

"Yes. What else? I've got to pick up my life somehow and carry on."

"I just wondered if you might like to borrow my little bungalow? The place Gareth used to call my wooden shack on the coast? It's small but it's cosy."

"Thanks, but I should go back."

"Why? You can work anywhere. There's Wi-Fi there but it's secluded. You're not going to have people knocking on the door feeling sorry for you.

12

You can stay as long as you like. I don't let it out like Mum and Dad used to."

Oh, it was so tempting! It would feel like a fresh start where nobody would know who she was or what she'd suffered.

"Ask me again in the morning," she said with her first smile since the last baking day.

That night, she collected together her working equipment and packed it away safely into storage boxes. She was a freelance illustrator and had worked for an advertising agency after university. Eventually she'd screwed up the courage to go it alone and had never regretted it. She loved working for herself. Loved the freedom to choose, the variety of the commissions, the fact that no two jobs were the same.

As she began sorting some clothes to take with her, she came upon one of Gareth's jumpers that he'd evidently just taken off and stuffed into the bottom of the wardrobe. She picked it up and buried her face in it. His own lovely scent lingered there yet. It was a musky, slightly sweaty smell that she loved. She drew in a deep breath, a big noseful, a massive lungful. If she shut her eyes he was there again. She mourned him, felt she had lost him, all over again. She was so tempted to pack the jumper and take it but the whole point of this little break was exactly that. To help her to break from her old life - her happy life. She folded it, returned it to the wardrobe and wiped her eyes.

Liz barely slept that night. Being in their old bed was impossible to consider so she went into the spare room and got into bed there. Her mind was a whirlwind. She was unable to settle to any train of thought and snippets of conversation from the afternoon collided with scenes from her early days, meeting Gareth and Miles for the first time, her first date with him. She gave up any attempt at sleeping and rose in the middle of the night to make tea. A hot shower freshened her up and she continued packing, assuming she would not be back for several days.

Miles rang early in the morning and offered to drop the keys and the address details around before work.

"I'm so grateful for this," she said. "Going away, starting to work again somewhere else, underlines the fact that my life's got to start again. If I gave in to my instincts I'd fold up somewhere and starve to death. I don't have any more ambitions. I don't want to live any longer and I don't think I'd have the strength to go on surrounded by the memories. He's everywhere in this house. I can still smell him, Miles. I'll have to cope without him eventually, but... I need to start somewhere."

She'd just made herself a hot drink when Miles called in briefly with a set of keys and a scribbled list of instructions for how to find his little weekend retreat. She knew he had bought it from his dad a few years back when he wanted to realise his capital to buy a winter home in Spain. It was one of a handful of small timber-clad single storey bungalows which dotted a narrow road leading to the sea. The road simply ended at a low cliff. Erosion had eaten away the land here on the East Riding coastline and the road itself continued to fall into the North Sea at a rate of yards per year.

Miles' bungalow, imaginatively named Sea Breezes, was about half a mile from the cliffs, though calling them that was brazen flattery. In places they reached eight or nine feet high, though here and there they swept down to beach level. Liz pulled her car in alongside the little house and stopped the engine. There were several of those single storey dwellings along the road. They were mainly painted in shades of green and she saw now exactly why Gareth called it a wooden shack.

There was a door to the front and another at the side, where she'd parked her car. She found the right key for this door which led straight into the kitchen, opened up and went inside. The place was compact but usefully laid out with two just-about-double bedrooms, lounge, the tiny galley kitchen she'd first entered and a bathroom/loo combo.

She hung her coat up and went back out to the car to bring in her case from the boot. Another trip out to the car saw all her luggage brought indoors.

The back window to the kitchen overlooked a small garden plot, mainly laid out to lawn. There were fields at the back and in the distance a big gas installation thrust its towers and scaffolding into the sky. The surroundings were so flat and the skies seemed massive. Today, they were grey, like her mood.

It took her very little time to put her things away and she gravitated to the kitchen to put the kettle on. Miles came most Sundays so the little kitchen was fairly well stocked with basics. She had called at the supermarket on the way and knelt to fill the fridge with fresh food and one of the cupboards with tins and packets. As the kettle clicked off she drowned a tea bag in boiling water, squeezed it with a spoon and hooked it out of the mug. She added a splash of milk and, grabbing the mug with both hands, she walked through into the living room. It contained a couple of two-seater sofas, one of which looked like it converted into a bed. There was little else in there but a wall of book-shelves, a coffee table and a very small flat-screen television.

It was barely lunchtime but Liz felt exhausted. Grief had worn her spirit thin and left her tired and wrung out. She fetched her laptop and her working materials into the living room then plugged in the computer and connected to the Wi-Fi. She blew across the top of her tea and sipped it. Its warmth was comforting. She so often felt cold now, though she didn't think it was just physical. She was cold to her soul. She checked her email, skipping through those which were sympathy messages. One day she would have to reply and thank people but not just now. Not while it was still so recent, so raw. She switched off again with a shuddering sigh.

She decided to make a sandwich and then have a walk on the beach. The day had turned out fine and sunny, but once she got to the shore she felt the wind cutting through her coat. The beach was sand with tongues of pebbles licking from the line of breakers towards the crouched brown cliffs of boulder clay.

She walked up the beach to the north first of all. She was going into the wind and hunched her shoulders, shoving her hands deep into her pockets as she did so. The logic was that on the way she would still have some residual warmth from the house but on the way back, when she had begun to be chilled, she would have the wind behind her. It was a piercing wind that felt like it could desiccate her skin over time. She walked slowly, almost mesmerised by the number and variety of pebbles on the beach. High up the strand, close to the low humps of cliffs, there were large flat cobbles. She could imagine them placed close together like a variegated crazy paving. The artist in her wanted to arrange them, to sort them and make a pathway to the bungalow door.

The tide was low at the moment and about half

way down the beach the pebbles were walnut-sized or smaller. They were preponderantly grey, drab, but here and there a bright stone stood out. She bent to pick out an orange one, then found herself smiling to realise it was water-worn brick. Miles had some books on beach pebbles back at the bungalow. She promised herself a read that evening. The tide was still ebbing and the stones she walked through were damp from the seawater. She loved the sucking, scrabbling sound as the foam retreated from the pebbles. She picked out a few pretty ones to take home and identify.

When she turned for home she realised that for the first time since it happened she had not been chewing away in her mind about Gareth's death. She felt almost light-hearted to realise that the world still had some interest for her. For the first time since that horrible Saturday she didn't wish she had died in the car with him. She slowly ambled along, zigzagging up and down and pausing to pick up anything that caught her fancy. She remembered seeing vinyl floor tiles printed with stones, for use in bathrooms. She could see why people would buy them. It was fascinating just staring into the heap and letting her mind see patterns, make connections. Almost back at the shattered road end, she stooped suddenly to pick up a gorgeously glowing green stone. It looked like a huge emerald. The colour was deep, dense and saturated. That was going in her little collection too.

Back inside the bungalow, Liz clicked the kettle switch and turned on the electric fire in the sitting room. She emptied out the stones from her jacket pocket onto a piece of kitchen towel. Her initial feeling was of deep disappointment. The glowing stones of her beach walk were mainly dull and powdery looking. Even her fabulous sea emerald looked lifeless now it had dried out. Oh well. She pulled a glass out of the cupboard by the sink, tipped the stones in and covered them with water. They lit up again glowing in the back light from the window. She smiled again. Something beautiful could always warm her heart.

Liz made tea and a sandwich and took them into the sitting room which was now cosy from the heat of the fire. She went across to the bookshelves to see what Miles had on offer, before she settled down. There was a clutch of Andy McNabs, the three Dragon Tattoo books, some James Patterson, a smattering of Lee Childs and a substantial collection of poetry books. He also had a number of natural history books; trees, pond life, birds and of course those connected with the seashore. These included books about seaweed and rock pools and, as she'd remembered, beach pebbles.

She settled herself in her favourite of the two sofas - the one which gave a view over the road and the field beyond. The light declined as she sank herself into the book. It helped her to identify most of her finds. The grey stuff was limestone and the pictures showed examples with fossils in. Most of the white, orange and yellow stones which looked so gorgeous wet but so dull when dry turned out to be quartz pebbles. You could polish them apparently - if you had the right equipment. There was a little section at the end which included material like her brick, industrial slag and glass. It turned out that her sumptuous sea emerald was probably a water-worn piece of glass, perhaps from a wine bottle. So much for glamour, she thought.

When she found herself dozing by the fire, she made up her mind to call it a day and go to bed. Physical tiredness from her walk into the wind helped her to fall asleep more easily than she had done for some time, although whenever she closed her eyes she saw pebbles.

Next morning Liz ate breakfast, washed up, then plugged in her laptop. Miles had emailed to ask if she minded him coming out there on Sunday as he usually did. If not, she could send him a shopping list and he'd drop by the supermarket Saturday evening. She sent a reply back to assure him that he must come and go as he pleased and asked for him to pick up a few things she'd forgotten. She also found a work commission in her inbox. Not a huge one but she was aware that with the passing of time she needed to earn some money. There'd be an insurance pay-out eventually but in the meantime she had a mortgage to pay on a single, erratic income.

She had been energised by the previous day's beach walk and she decided she would incorporate a beach-combing session into her daily routine. Miles would be coming tomorrow so she thought she'd see if she could find any more interesting pebbles to show him. This morning, though, she'd get to grips with that new commission. The light in the second bedroom was best so she set up her drawing board and materials in there, aware that she'd have to move them before Miles arrived.

Two weeks had passed since the unthinkable had happened and for the first time she began to feel purposeful again. She couldn't have planned for a situation in which she was widowed at twenty-eight years of age. How can you start to think of your widowhood when you are still trying to decide when to have your children? Work was definitely helping. Because part of her mind was occupied with planning and executing the physical task, she wasn't dwelling on her loss to the extent she had been. It was too soon, too early, to assume she was healing and coping, though. She just did whatever it took to get through the day.

After lunch, she went back into the second bedroom and scrutinised her morning's work. It was good and she was happy to award herself an afternoon walk. Scrambling down to the shore, she once again decided to walk north. A couple of times, she stopped to collect what she recognised from her reading as fossils. One was a bullet-shaped belemnite and another a bit of coral, though it didn't look much like the modern ones. Again, though she now recognised it as worthless, she bent to collect a couple of pieces of the smoothed green glass. She also picked up some seaweed. It was the sort she knew as bladder wrack. Wasn't it supposed to help you tell the weather? Or was that fir cones? She marvelled at her own ignorance.

Once she'd returned to the bungalow, Liz cooked and ate a meal then trawled through the books again. She found a novel and tried to get interested but she was so tired. It was a combination of the fresh air, a full stomach and the fact that she was simply exhausted from a fortnight of restless nights. She took the book and a cup of tea to bed and soon fell into a deep sleep.

3

Miles came early on Sunday and brought a box of groceries with him. He unpacked the things Liz had asked for and half a dozen bottles of wine. He protested when she got her purse out and said all he was doing was restocking the bungalow.

"If that's what you're doing, and you're letting me use it, then you've got to let me pay you rent!'

"Rubbish!" he said. "You're my friend. Gareth was my best friend." He gave her a hollow, haunted look and bit his lip. She thought he was going to cry and if he did, she knew that she would too. "Anyway," he continued, "you're acting as caretaker. I owe you for that."

"Rubbish!" she replied, and they laughed half-heartedly.

They prepared some vegetables and Liz put a joint in the oven, then they both set off for a walk. This time they walked south. Miles told her about most of the pebbles which she picked up and eventually dropped. He also pointed out some low concrete structures on the beach in the distance.

"These were cliff-top pillboxes and gun

emplacements from the war. So much of the cliff has been washed away since then."

He laughed at her for collecting the green glass. There wasn't much - maybe a couple of pieces each time she walked the beach - but she leapt on it with delight. He passed her a piece but she didn't consider that one good enough.

"Oh, I don't like that stuff," she said. "It's such a mucky green. I like this colour. Just this particular shade." She held her sea emeralds up to the light to show him.

"Merlot!" he stated with a knowing nod.

They returned to the bungalow to the rich smell of roast lamb and Liz put the vegetables on to cook while Miles laid the table and set out glasses. Over the meal they naturally returned to the subject of Gareth and the mystery of his blood alcohol level.

"Why would he do that, though?" Liz puzzled. She looked at the red wine in her own glass. "He liked a whisky - hell, you know that! You also know that he never drank when he was driving. They say he had most of that bottle inside him. I just can't believe it."

"I don't know what to say, Liz. I think he had a lot on his mind. He had more going on in his life than he wanted to face."

"What do you mean? Was he worried about something? What do you know about it, Miles? I'm his wife... was his wife... I should have known if he had problems. Are you keeping something from me?" Her voice had become higher pitched, gabbled.

"I'm not sure. I just get the feeling he was disturbed about something. I'm still trying to figure this out. When I've got something tangible, something sensible, I'll tell you."

He leant over to refill her glass but she shook her head and put her hand over the top, thinking of Gareth's determination to lose his mind completely in drink and effectively drive himself into a tree... The thought shook her up. Was it deliberate?

"Was it suicide, Miles?" Her voice was suddenly choked, tiny.

"It was uncharacteristic, that's all I feel safe saying," he answered. "Who ever knows what's happening in someone else's mind?"

"But he was my husband! I should have known. Should have guessed!"

Miles finished the bottle and they talked the subject around and across but eventually they both felt too tired to take it any further. Liz moved her work and drawing board from the second bedroom so Miles could sleep there. He was only staying the one night. The unaccustomed alcohol, added to the wearing effect of a fortnight's grief meant, she slept heavily and woke late. Miles left after breakfast in order to get to work.

Liz worked again in the morning. She found that she fell into old work habits and the concentration on physical activities kept the surface of her mind engaged. She didn't dwell overtly on her loss but her body, her soul, felt hollow. There was a black hole inside her into which all hope, all comfort, disappeared. She worked on until lunchtime when she stopped for a quick sandwich.

After eating, she put on her boots and went for a walk down the lane instead of on the beach. The fields were flat and featureless. In places, the hedgerows had been ripped out to procure another few square yards of harvest. It meant that the wind met with no resistance and the few thorn bushes leant sharply in the direction of the prevailing blasts. Liz walked for an hour and turned back when she began to feel chilled. By the time she got back to the bungalow she was grateful for the electric fire which warmed her quickly.

She put a casserole in the oven, brewed a pot of tea and sat by the fire with another of Miles' books. This was a poetry anthology so that when her mind wandered she could stop. When dusk fell like soot out of the air, she dished up her casserole and, throwing over her usual caution, she opened one of the bottles of red Miles had unpacked yesterday. It was full-bodied and felt more like a comfort food than a drink. The rich, hearty beef casserole really hit the spot and, with the glass of wine, made her feel sleepy.

She curled up on the sofa and nodded off. When

she woke the night was well advanced. She sat up and went to pour herself another glass of red. She cupped it between her hands as she stood looking over the moonlit road, wondering what time it was but not caring enough to find out. As she sipped the wine she thought about her life now. It seemed pointless. She envisaged day after day rolling by as the last couple had, tedious in themselves and fading into a grey future. What did she have left to live for? She gulped back the contents of the glass and refilled it.

Liz felt like a castaway on an island. This was a peninsula here so it might as well be an island. Oh, she could just go home certainly, but the isolation, the sense of solitariness, was within her. She carried her own bitter loneliness wherever she went. Emptying the last of the bottle's contents into her glass, she took it with her into the kitchen where she ripped a page from the shopping list pad. She drank the wine back and grabbed a pen.

"HELP! I have just been widowed, aged 28, and my life is over." She looked at it and added her name and email address then folded the note and wrapped it in a small polythene sandwich bag. She retrieved the empty bottle from the sitting room, pushed the plastic wrapped message inside and screwed the top back on.

Without pausing to put on her coat, Liz rushed out of the kitchen door and down the cut-off lane to the beach. She teetered across the dark sand and tide-washed pebbles and, through a curtain of tears, she yelled, "My life is over! I'm dead! I've got nothing to live for!" Pulling her arm back she hurled the green bottle as far into the moon-kissed waves as she could then fell to her knees, sobbing.

Liz knelt in the foam, her knees soaked, her heart in shreds, until her teeth chattered and her body ached with cold. She felt she wanted to throw herself forward and embrace the black waves; to lie there forever and forget. Reluctantly she drew herself upright and staggered and dripped her way in the darkness back to the bungalow. Her thinking was awry and she began to wonder why she'd thrown the message into the waves. Who did she expect would find it? If it survived, if it came ashore somewhere, if anyone even read it, would they contact her? Did it, as she now wondered, sound like the ravings of a mad woman? Who'd reply to that?

She stripped off her dripping clothes, ran a hot bath and soaked the chill out of her bones. She was so tired, so dizzy with alcohol and grief, that she dozed in the warm water, jerking suddenly awake, unsure of where she was. Eventually, as the water cooled, she dragged herself out of the bath, rubbed herself dry and shuffled into the bedroom where she crawled between the sheets and fell into a heavy sleep.

***

Liz woke in the grey dawn light with a dull, aching head, a sour stomach and a huge thirst. What had she been thinking to rush out last night with that ridiculous message in a bottle? She felt hot embarrassment at the thought of somebody reading the scribbled note that she'd hurled into the sea in the depths of last night's despair. She still felt as hollow, empty and grey as she did yesterday but the morning light, murky as it was, made her feel she had a future, albeit a lonely one.

Over the next few days she dropped into the comfortable habit of working in the morning, walking the beach in the afternoon and either doing some more work if it was going well, or selecting one of Miles' books and settling down to read. Every beach walk allowed her to add another one or two pieces of deep green glass to her collection.

The commissions and consequently the fees kept coming in but Liz knew it didn't even come close to the mortgage payments. She began to think seriously that she may have to sell the house. Previously she'd have said she couldn't bear to lose the house she had shared with Gareth. Now, though, she feared the thought of walking through the rooms there would drive her mad. She'd expect to see him through every doorway, strain to hear his footsteps climbing the stairs. The reality of his absence was so much worse than her darkest imagination could have conjured.

She decided that next weekend she would return to the town with Miles and go to see an estate agent. A flat would do. One like Miles' own two-bedded apartment would be ideal. On a whim she emailed him and suggested she accompany him back to town next Sunday night. She'd have to go back to her old house eventually but she appreciated this time out of time. It allowed her to pretend she'd left her real life behind, and distance herself from it. Certainly, she had left behind the enquiries of anxious friends and the over-solicitous fussing of her mother, however kindly meant.

Yes, if Miles would allow her another few weeks' grace here, she would go back to town to a new home and a new, though diminished, life. What she really wanted was to go back to somebody else's life; somebody who hadn't lost her dearest love. Liz took some deep breaths and mentally shook herself, steeled herself to endure rather than enjoy her future.

4

On Friday night Liz was browsing the bookshelves looking for something not too taxing for the last hour before she settled down to sleep. She spotted a book of First World War poems and pulled it down from the shelf. She opened the book with a feeling of familiarity. It was the same anthology they had on their own shelves at home and one which Gareth used to pick up and leaf through often. Liz opened it at random and read a few words. Its tone of stoical sadness and determination chimed with her own mood. After half an hour or so of moving from one poem to another she turned to the front of the book and her heart momentarily soared then plummeted.

On the flyleaf was Gareth's unmistakable writing; spiky, not-quite-italic, stylish. Seeing it brought her up short; it was such a shock. A bigger shock, though, was what he had written.

To my darling Miles.
Enjoy these poems of men at their best.
With all my heart, Gareth.

Liz dropped the book on her lap and her hands leapt to her cheeks. My darling? All my heart? What did it mean? Oh, she knew exactly what the bloody hell it meant but she couldn't believe it. She didn't want to believe it. Gareth and Miles? When? How? How long? Actually, they'd known one another longer than she'd known them. They roomed together in first year. Back then had they been lovers?

She cast back, trying to remember how things were in those early days. She met Gareth, got on well with him and they began to go out together. They went around rather casually at first, as friends, with a group of others. Did the group include Miles from the start? She thought it might have. She hadn't noticed any particular vibe between them. Was her husband gay? How could he be? How could she not know?

Miles, in all the intervening years, had never had a girlfriend. He wasn't the kind of man she thought of as being obviously gay, though. He didn't have any effete mannerisms. Actually, she wasn't aware of knowing any gay men and her knowledge of homosexuals came largely from the television and films. Often they were caricatures, she knew. But *Gareth*? Yes, he was a good-looking man. She could imagine a gay man might fancy him too. What she couldn't imagine was that Gareth would fancy another man.

He loved *her*. There was no doubt in her mind about that. Surely she'd know if he loved Miles too? Wouldn't she? Hang on, though. They had spent so much time together. Was it unusual for two men who worked together all day to spend a day of their weekend together too? She hadn't questioned it before. Maybe she should have done. And Miles had been a bit evasive when she'd asked whether Gareth had been worrying about anything.

She switched on her laptop and emailed Miles.

To: Miles
From: Me

Miles - tell me about you and Gareth.

Liz

She was tempted to leave her inbox open and wait for him to reply. He had a smartphone and she could usually guarantee to get a quick answer from him. She didn't want to sit there, though, twitching with anxiety, just waiting for him to get back to her. She turned it off and went back to the bookshelves. Her eye was drawn to any book of which they also had a copy. She pulled them down and checked the front pages in case there were any more gifts from Gareth. Only *The Rubaiyat of Omar Khayyam* had an inscription in Gareth's hand. This was dated the

Christmas of the year before she went up to university. The year the men had shared rooms. It said, 'Happy Christmas, dearest Miles. Love from Gareth.' It seemed to her more than a man would normally write to a man. They must have been lovers in their first year.

Liz went over and over their early meetings, her first knowledge of Miles. Had there been any sign? A quick check on her email - no reply - and she went to bed.

Her sleep was fitful and troubled that night. For once, Miles had failed to reply within an hour or so and she thought, no she *knew*, that it was because there really was something to tell about the situation between him and her late husband. There was a story to tell and he didn't know how to tell it. Or maybe didn't want to. How could he avoid telling her, though? She was his friend, she was – how did she even think her way around this mess? – she was his lover's wife!

She'd heard or read stories about people whose husband or wife had died and then they'd found out about a secret lover. It had always been a rival of the same sex, though. She knew how to hate a woman who had enticed Gareth away from her. She could really dig her teeth and claws into the knowledge that he'd been playing away from home with some floozy. But how did you even think about it when your husband had been in love with another man? A

34

man you yourself liked and respected as a friend?

Her mind whirled with possibilities; with the knowledge that she didn't understand a huge part of her late husband's heart and soul. She needed to speak with Miles. Maybe in the morning he would have found a way to tell her. Maybe there'd be a message in her inbox when she woke. Eventually, beyond exhaustion, she slept.

5

It was still dark on that Saturday morning when she was awoken by a loud knocking on the door and then the sound of a key in the lock. Oh God! Miles. It had to be him. He had the only other key and a burglar wouldn't unlock the door. Why the hell couldn't he just email? She could have a good row in an email but she hated confrontation. Still, she'd asked for it, more or less summoning him. She scrabbled her way out of bed and bundled herself into her dressing gown.

"Miles? Is that you?"

"Liz - I had to come and talk to you," he shouted. It sounded as if he'd come in via the kitchen and she could hear him putting the kettle on and clattering crockery around. She wanted answers but, now he was here, she was nervous. She wanted to postpone the moment of confrontation. Really, in her heart, she feared an argument. She hated fighting. She couldn't go in there now. How could she look into his eyes as if everything were normal? Shower. She'd have a shower. That would put it off for a bit.

"Let me get showered and dressed and I'll come

through and talk."

Liz quickly got cleaned up and threw yesterday's clothes back on so she could go through and meet Miles. She couldn't put it off any longer. She had to grasp the nettle and get stuck into the business of finding out the truth. In the kitchen, she saw that he had put a plate of toast in the middle of the table with butter and jars of jam, marmalade and marmite alongside it. He was fidgeting with the cutlery, evidently nervous too.

"Oh, breakfast! Thank God!" she said, pulling out a chair and starting to fiddle with the toast and the spreads. Anything to defer the confrontation ahead. Miles placed a mug of tea in front of her. She picked up a slice of toast, smeared it lightly with butter and opened a jar of raspberry jam. She began spreading and talking at once.

"Are you going to stay the whole weekend? It would be lovely if you did – company for two days?"

"Liz. You're gabbling. You're nervous. There's no need to be. Just take it easy. Eat your toast and drink your tea then we'll talk."

"Sorry, yes, I'm as nervous as hell." She put her untouched toast back on the plate. "I don't think I can eat this, sorry."

"Don't worry," he said. "To be honest I wanted something to do. I couldn't just pace up and down while I waited for you. Mind you, I'm hungry now. I set off early to come here and I've not eaten. I have a feeling I'll need some sustenance for this."

At last, Liz looked up and held his gaze.

"I know that you must realise from my email that I have an idea what there was between you and Gareth – my husband." Why had she said that? They both knew who Gareth was – and it was evident that he was not simply her husband.

"Yes. I think you've got more than an idea. Let's just finish up here and then we'll sit in the comfortable chairs. If you're not too horrified – if you don't hate me – I'll stay tonight and go Sunday evening. I don't really know how I expect you to react, though. We're both in new territory here. We'll have to play this entirely by ear." He flashed a thin ghost of a smile as he began buttering his own slice of toast.

Uncomfortably, in a silence more brittle and edgy than is usual for such old friends, they finished breakfast, which in the event, Liz hardly touched, and left the dishes in the sink. She followed Miles into the little sitting room and took her place on her favourite sofa. Miles sat on the other.

"So. You know." It was a simple statement; no hint of a question.

"Yes. I want to know a lot more about it, though. I feel on very shaky ground, Miles. I didn't know about this... this fundamental aspect of my husband's sexuality. I didn't have a clue. I never before thought of you as my rival but you were."

"No, Liz. I couldn't compete with you. I know I couldn't. So how did you find out?"

She got to her feet, opened the poetry book at the front page and held it out to him.

"Ah. Bugger. I never thought of that. I keep it here because I didn't want to leave it in my flat to be found. I'd just forgotten."

"So tell me."

He sat back in the cushions of the sofa and gazed at the wall. He seemed unable to meet her eyes.

"Gosh. Where do I start? I first realised I was… gay at school. They say everyone, straight or gay, goes through a phase of being attracted to the same sex but it wasn't a phase with me. I had friends who were girls but never a girlfriend. When it came to sexual thoughts, to…" Miles cleared his throat, "to… erm, you know… I always thought of boys. By the time I went to Uni I knew for sure I was gay. I thought my birthdays had all come at once when Gareth turned up in my digs as the extra student. He was, well, I don't need to tell you." He looked at her then. "You thought he was someone special too."

At this, Miles looked down at his hands and blushed. She hadn't expected him to react that way; to be so shy about it. She wasn't the only one burning with embarrassment.

"Did you…" She paused, not knowing how to say what she was thinking. "Did you seduce him?"

she asked, surprised by the primness of her question.

He looked at her as if judging her state of mind.

"I didn't need to. You know what the body language is like between people who fancy each other. The little looks, glances, secret smiles. The small touches of the hand; the way you sometimes biff one another on the arm because, hey, it's physical contact and you're bursting for it, however it happens?"

"Was it like that with you and Gareth?"

"Slow to start off with and I was afraid to make any overt advances in case I frightened him off. But you can just tell, can't you?"

"Did you... hell, it's so awkward, this. Did you have sex – make love – consummate your relationship?" She glanced up at Miles and found herself blushing furiously. "Sorry. Whatever way I try to say it, things come out sounding prissy and judgemental. I'm not judging but I'm feeling dreadfully hurt and I'm really finding it difficult to understand. Hell, there I go again. I don't mean I don't understand homosexuality. Well, I don't from experience but I understand it as a concept – a lifestyle choice."

"Lifestyle choice? Liz, do you really think I chose this? That I chose to be... how can I put this? That I chose to be someone different from all my friends, someone people mistrust, misunderstand, hate, even? Why would anyone choose *that*? Choose to be cut off. Choose loneliness."

"I didn't mean it like that!" Liz looked aghast. "All I meant was that you can choose to live as a gay couple… to… come out, or whatever you call it. That's the choice I meant."

"I suppose I know what you mean. It's just… people talk as if we had any say in the matter. I didn't choose to be gay any more than I chose my brown hair and grey eyes. We did choose to… how can I put it? To express our love. We weren't out to anyone but each other but I know we would have been, after we'd graduated. If you…"

"If I hadn't come long and stolen him."

"Oh, it felt like that at the time, I admit. But I just had to 'man up'." He flashed a sad little smile at her.

"I'm doing my best here, Miles. I can understand how you loved him… because I did too. I can even see…" she cleared her throat then plunged on, "I can see what he saw in you. You're a good-looking man and a lovely person. What I don't get is how Gareth could have loved you and then within a few weeks or months gone on to tell me that he loved me?"

"It happens, Liz. I thought I had it all when we finally told one another of our feelings. I really thought I had a potential partner for life. I knew he loved me. I just didn't realise he was one of those people capable of loving both men and women. When you appeared on the scene and joined our larger social group, I never thought I'd lose him to

41

you. You can't imagine how I felt when I saw him begin to get close to you. I couldn't believe it at first. I thought he was just trying to appear straight. He wasn't, though. He was bisexual and only just finding that out for himself."

"Since I found out, I've been seeing this just from my viewpoint, Miles," Liz said. "I never realised that you must have felt betrayed."

"I was gutted, Liz. When I realised Gareth was more than just a friend to you I was bitterly jealous. To do him justice, Gareth told me himself. That's a night I'll never forget! I thought I'd die of alcohol poisoning for one thing. He told me that he still loved me. That he knew he would always love me. You see, Liz, we had something more than just a physical attraction. More than just friendship. We shared a lot of our deepest beliefs and hopes. I thought I had found my soul-mate and had him stolen away."

"Like I just have! I don't believe this, Miles! You're making yourself out to be the great loser here. I'm the one who's lost her husband at 28 years of age!"

"Sorry, of course you have. Nobody's lost as much as you but you're not the only one who's lost him. I'm just trying to be honest with you, Liz. I felt kicked in the guts. I'd made it obvious that I was in love with Gareth. That I was prepared to make him my life. To make his future my future. Towards the end of first year it all looked as though it would happen. He told me he felt the same. We had a season, that summer term and the long vac, when my life had never been so saturated in bliss. It never has since. I saw my future mapped out before me and it included happiness. Then along came a rival. You."

"I never knew, Miles." They sat, each staring at the carpet. Not knowing what to say, Liz leapt to her feet as though to deflect the embarrassment of the moment. "Let's have a cuppa. Tea or coffee this time?"

"What? Oh, anything… whatever you're having." His voice was subdued.

She made a good deal of noise in the kitchen, to drown any possible sound he might make. Thoughts, ideas and questions chased one another through her roiling mind. She was sure Miles was the same and she just wanted, for a few moments, to take a break from it all; to lose herself in the task of making hot drinks and postpone what she knew would be more, and possibly more painful, revelations from her husband's 'best friend'. She felt naïve; like a silly girl who hadn't been able to see what was in front of her face all this time.

When she came back into the sitting room with a laden tea-tray, she was acutely, hotly embarrassed to realise that in her absence Miles had been crying. He didn't attempt to wipe the tears away.

"Here, get yourself round this," she said, handing him one of the mugs.

"So. I was the enemy?"

"Not at first," he said. You were one of the gang - funny, clever, a good mate. I didn't expect it would turn into more. I didn't see it coming. By the time I saw you holding hands, saw his eyes glowing, and worst of all, heard him talk about you, I knew I'd lost him. He confessed, right up front. He told me he wanted to get married. That he'd never met a girl he felt like that about. You know Gareth, though. He hadn't a cruel bone in his body. He kept telling me he still loved me - that he'd always love me. That spring term, when the two of you were a pair, I don't know how I kept it all together. I began by being bitterly jealous but in a childish, 'It's not fair,' kind of way. I couldn't fight you. I couldn't compete. If it were another man Gareth had taken up with, I could try to be the better man, to win him back. But when he wanted a wife, children, there was nothing I could do. I was lost."

Fresh tears flowed down Miles' cheeks. It looked to Liz as though, in his imagination, he had lost Gareth to her all over again.

"I can't believe I didn't know any of this was going on!" Liz was appalled at her own blindness.

"You were too happy to see beyond your own situation," Miles said. "We'd been discreet about our love affair. It would have become common knowledge eventually. I like to believe we'd have been proud enough of each other to come out, to shout about it."

"Gareth never gave the slightest hint. I can't believe that he'd keep quiet about something, someone, who meant so much." She suddenly held up her hands in a placating gesture. "Oh God, Miles! I'm so sorry. That sounded as if I don't believe that he loved you. It explains his moodiness at times. The fact that he was sometimes so withdrawn and didn't want to talk to me about it."

"I didn't want to say any of this before, Liz… before you found out, that is. But I've wondered how he coped all these years. He and I still loved each other very much. We had our Saturday afternoons together and, of course, we spent much of our time at work in one another's company."

"Were you still… actively in love? Still having a… physical… relationship?"

"No, but that was part of the problem. When he got engaged to you he made up his mind to stay faithful to you. That meant that certainly I, and I suspect he, fought constantly against our nature. The times we've spent alone in one another's company just about having to sitting on our hands – we were in a situation of maximum temptation. It would have been less of a problem if I didn't like you so much, Liz. You weren't just my rival. You were my mate too. It was bloody difficult!"

"Do you suppose that was what he was worried about recently? You know, when I asked if you knew what was on his mind and you went kind of shifty."

"Shifty?"

"Yeah. You said you couldn't say anything for sure but you'd let me know when you had more than a vague idea."

Miles studied his fingernails as if they were fascinating then raised his eyes to meet hers.

"I know that for us both, temptation was getting harder to resist. We both knew we wanted to renew the physical side of our relationship. But Gareth had another goal in mind. He kept talking about 'just a few years' time' when you'd made a name for yourself in your career and you'd be in a position to put things on hold for a while. He so desperately wanted to be a father, Liz. I just had an overwhelming desire and lust - and love for him - to fight against. That was bloody hard enough." Miles wiped his face with one hand. "He had all that but he was pulled in two ways. He wanted you, too. He loved, needed, lusted after you and he so wanted to be a dad. I think in the end it pulled him apart."

"You mean you think he *did* kill himself? It was deliberate?"

"Oh… I don't know if I'd call it suicide but at the very least, he didn't care if he died."

"Or who he left behind! Or how they would feel about it. Or if he killed anyone else!" Liz knew she was beginning to sound querulous, bitter, hysterical even, but her hurt, her shock, at the situation she'd simply never imagined began to seep through the cracks. "I don't know what to think now, Miles. Did he really love me or did he love you all along and I was just a handy womb? His ticket to fatherhood?"

6

"Come on. Grab your coat. Let's go and see if we can get you a bit more green glass. A blow on the beach before lunch will do us both good." Miles stood in a single elegant movement and helped Liz to her feet. They both got their outdoor gear on and marched down the lane towards the shore.

"You were certainly not just Gareth's means to having a child, Liz. I could tell from the off how much he loved you. He used to look at you the way he looked at me before you came along. I guess the thing is, once you truly love someone, you stay in love with him and then if you find another person you love – you don't have to un-love the first. He did really love us both." Miles scuffed up stones with his trainers. The pebbles lay in patches where they had swept in from the sea.

"You don't have a finite amount of love in your heart so that you have to halve it if you love two people. Love grows to fit the number of people you need it for. I knew about you, knew who I was sharing him with, but you could never know about me. That was the theory anyway."

Liz walked on, slightly ahead, still reluctant to hear what he had to say but drawn to it nonetheless. She shrugged against the wind and stuffed her hands into her coat pockets. The wind, coming from the sea, was shredding the foam on top of the breakers and hurling it at her. She felt the spray on her face as she lifted it to gaze up the beach.

"I wonder what would have happened if he'd not died?"

"If only… 'If only' thoughts don't really help. We could talk ourselves round in circles wondering."

"You think you'd have become lovers again, don't you?" Her voice went soft and small and he had to strain to hear it against the wind.

"I hoped so. I always hoped so. But he was determined to be faithful, although I know it was hard for him. I think that was the struggle that broke him that Saturday. He couldn't take it, he bought the whisky and… I don't know… We'll never know if it was a deliberate attempt to kill himself or if he just got so drunk he lost control of the car. My own feeling is that he intended to get to my place in such a state that his inhibitions were trashed and he'd let himself give in. Then he could tell himself it wasn't his fault; it was because he was so rat-arsed he didn't know what he was doing."

In spite of everything, the hurt and the grief and missing Gareth so much, Liz found herself giggling at the rather formal Miles saying 'rat-arsed' then she stopped herself short. She feared she'd become hysterical if she let herself laugh.

"What?" Miles heard the titter and turned to her, a smile on his own face.

"Just the way you said it," she smiled in return.

He reached towards her and put an arm around her shoulder and she leaned in to him and rested her head on his. That little laugh they'd shared, trivial and silly as it really was, had broken the tension and restored their old friendship and trust. She put her arms around him and he reached around her with both of his. They hugged one another tightly in the knowledge that they had each lost the one man they both loved with all their hearts. She didn't want them to lose each other too.

"Come on – let's find something good on this beach!" he said, breaking the embrace and trudging up and down one of the oval sweeps of pebbles stretching from the water-line up the sand. They each stooped several times to pick something up but as often as not, discarded it straight away.

"Hey, look at this!" Miles called to Liz as she wandered up the beach.

"What? What have you got?!"

"See this little orange one? It's a carnelian. That's classed as semi-precious. You can find them set into jewellery."

"Oh, isn't it gorgeous? It looks like a sucked jelly baby! Sort of translucent. Oh, bring that back to the bungalow, won't you?"

"Haha! Me with my carnelians and you with your manky bits of glass. Who'll get rich first?"

"Neither of us because all we'll do is stick them on your kitchen windowsill!"

They linked arms like the old friends they were and wandered back to the bungalow to get something to eat. Now the shock had dissipated, Liz didn't feel so edgy about Miles. Now and then she still thought with slight horror about what Miles and Gareth had actually got up to. It was so outside of her own experience. She still couldn't square it with the Gareth she knew and loved but it was undeniable that he was bisexual and if it had to be with anyone, somehow, possibly stupidly, it felt better that it was with someone she also liked and respected.

"At least I don't feel so bad about this as I did when it was just me on my own grieving about him," she told Miles over a quick meal. "Somehow it's a trouble shared."

"Are you sure you wouldn't be better staying with your parents for a few weeks, Liz? I'm sure things feel worse when you're on your own."

"Hell, no! It's worse at night of course; that's when I miss him so much. Just the memory of stretching out my legs to feel him there next to me. Putting an arm out to touch him. But the worst time... Ha! You'll laugh!"

"Go on, try me."

"Recently, only a few nights ago, I opened one of those bottles of wine. I was just going to have a glass with my dinner but you know how it is? Your caution goes by the time you're half way down the glass."

"So go on. What did you do?"

They took the plates through and began washing up as they talked. Talk flowed much easier now that they could relax again in one another's company.

"I fell asleep, then woke some time in the night. I finished the wine off, feeling pathetic and sorry for myself. I feel really embarrassed to think of it now." She told him about writing the note and throwing it into the sea. She glanced up to see how he was taking it. Miles was smiling at her.

"What'll you do if someone finds it? If they get in touch?"

"Do you think there's much chance?"

"Not a lot. I think it's more likely that your bottle will smash on the rocks somewhere, or on one of those bits of old wartime concrete stuff that's all over the east coast. It'll become more of that green, sea-worn glass you're always picking up!"

"Even if it survives and is opened, they've only got my email address. I'd delete it straight away. Honestly, I'd be too embarrassed to read the thing. I mean, what would they say? There's no answer to 'Help, my life is over.' If it is, they couldn't do anything. I'd have topped myself. If it isn't over, if I've come through it, then why do I need a reply?"

7

Next morning they spent a couple of hours on the beach, Liz learning lots more about the stones she picked up. She now had quite a collection of her 'sea emeralds' which Miles loved to poke fun at. He gave her half a dozen or so carnelian and agate pebbles which she noticed still held some of their shine even after the seawater had dried up from their surface. On the kitchen sill she had a half pint glass almost full of the green fragments and a saucer with the agates and carnelians that Miles had found. Some of the agates had bands or stripes in them, subtle and attractive.

Liz checked her email and found another query about a job, which she thought she'd take on. She parcelled up the one she'd finished and prepared it for the post. That afternoon they would go back into town. She toyed with getting a lift from Miles and returning on the bus but they were so infrequent she decided to take her own car. She didn't want to risk missing the last bus and having to spend the night at her old home alone. In any case, Miles suggested, almost insisted, that she stay at his flat that night and go to the estate agent's first thing Monday morning.

She went back that afternoon to the home she'd shared with Gareth and stood on the step for a few moments, clutching the key in her hand. She swallowed hard and dashed a tear away from her cheek. Was it ridiculous to feel so nervous? Yet the minute she let herself in the front door and shifted the junk mail from the mat, she knew she had to sell up. It was unbearable to look into the rooms where she expected to see Gareth. Going into their bedroom was the worst. She really couldn't sleep here anymore. She gathered up some more clothes and stuffed them into a bag. Putting it into the back of the car, she pulled away and made for Miles' flat. There they discussed her decision to sell up and she thought she might as well use the estate agent who'd sold them the house so few years previously.

In the morning she left the agent a key and arranged for him to take photographs, put the house on the market and send her details of smaller properties. No point in trying to pack up her stuff now. She'd get a removal company to do all that when the time came. For a fee, the agents would show prospective buyers around the house too, freeing her up from the headache of selling.

She drove back out to the coast and, with a feeling of relief, once again unlocked the door to the bungalow and made for the kettle. She fixed herself a sandwich and took the plate and her drink through to the sitting room. As she usually did on her return, she switched on the laptop and read her mail. Her heart thumped when she saw one from a sender she didn't recognise. The subject line read, 'Message in a bottle'.

Liz put her mug down on the coffee table with a shaking hand. What had she told Miles? That she'd bin it without reading it? At the time, she'd really meant that. Yet the nosy part of her soul couldn't resist just a peek at what was inside. She'd read it and bin it. How bad could that be? She laughed to herself. The phrase, 'What could possibly go wrong?' tickled its way through her mind.

She clicked on the message to open it.

From: Judith Gower
To: Me

I'm just messaging you to tell you that I found your bottle this morning. I live near the coast in Lincolnshire and I was walking along the beach with my brother when we saw this green thing up on the tide line. We had to smash it open to get at the message. You sounded desperately unhappy when you wrote that. There was no date but I hope enough time has passed for you to gain a little balance in your life. It's a terrible thing to lose your partner so young.

Let me tell you a bit about me. I'm a teacher, I'm 34 and

56

I'm divorced. See, I know about losing a partner, though not in the same way of course. I lost mine in a very hurtful and messy way and I lost my home, the man I thought was my best friend, and a good deal of my faith in human nature, all at the same time. I thought my life was over too. I was wrong and I do so much hope that you are wrong too.

If you feel a little better, maybe you'll reply and let me know how you're doing? I feel a bit worried about you, although we don't know one another. Look after yourself. You are your own best asset and resource.

Judith Gower

Liz stared at the screen. She read the email three times then logged off and shut down the computer, as though to distance herself as much as possible from… from what? A kind stranger who was moved by her plight? Someone who'd recognised another person's suffering and responded? No. She was trying to escape from that shameful drunken outburst of self-pity which had resulted in her throwing the message into the sea in the dead of night. Even the next morning she'd known she'd embarrassed herself.

Liz knew she was dithering. She started peeling and chopping vegetables. She got some meat out of the freezer and put it to defrost, then made another coffee. She even peered through the door into the sitting room and looked at the laptop as if it were a malevolent beast, crouching on the sofa and waiting to leap upon her.

"Oh, this is bloody ridiculous!" she actually said aloud, then laughed at herself.

Turning the laptop back on, she opened the email and read it again. Its tone was encouraging, reassuring. She decided she'd reply. She'd do it now, on the whim and hope she didn't regret it as much as she'd regretted the original message.

To: Judith Gower
From: Me

I'm not sure how to reply to you except to thank you very much for responding to a cry from the heart. I'm embarrassed to remember the state I was in (I'd emptied that bottle by myself!) the night I threw that message into the sea. My husband was killed in a road accident a few weeks ago at the age of 29. There are complicated issues I have to get my head around too. I'm working again – I'm an illustrator – and I think that's saving my sanity.

I'm sorry to hear about your divorce. Even an amicable divorce is the breaking of dreams. It sounds as though yours was very far from this.

Thank you for taking the trouble to reach out to my cry for help. Originally I wished I hadn't thrown the message into the sea. Now, I'm glad that you are the person who found it.

Liz Ellis

She read it through again, hesitated, then hit 'Send' and closed down the computer. Back in the kitchen she continued with her preparations for dinner, her mind still whirling around the fact that someone had replied. It could have been any idiot who'd picked that bottle up. Someone who might have cyber-stalked her and made her regret that she'd ever reached out for help. She'd probably never hear from this woman again but even if she did, her kindly tone, the fact they weren't too distant in age, acted as reassurance.

Over the next few days, Liz continued to find small jobs pouring in to her inbox and they kept her busy and her mind occupied. She still managed to find time for a little walk on the shore each day, though. It had come to be a welcome time of reflection for her. She still couldn't believe how lonely she felt, every day, every minute, in spite of the fact that she and Miles had now re-established their old, comfortable, friendly relationship and they emailed back and forth each day. Yet the daily march up and down the beach, when the surface of her mind was busily sorting stones, allowed the deeper parts to worry over her future and settle a few things.

Initially she had felt she was taking advantage of Miles' kindness in using the bungalow as her home for the duration. She began to realise, though, that in his own way he was making reparation for being the third party in their marriage. There was no need for him to feel that way, she reasoned. She'd come along as the third person when Miles had thought his dreams had been fulfilled. All the time, as she raked the situation over in her brain, she was seeing, comparing, choosing, the stones from the shingle of the beach. With time, she became more adept at picking out the agates and carnelians. However, she couldn't walk past the bright green and just leave it there. Her collection grew. Was that windowsill going to be big enough?

By the weekend she had heard from Judith a second time. It was just a brief note but it touched her nonetheless.

From: Judith Gower
To: Me

Hi, Liz. Hope you don't mind me making contact again? I'm a chatty person! Can't help myself. Do you live by the sea? I'm not too far but not really on the coast. In fact we only go every couple of weeks, just for a blow. It's such a coincidence that I found your message. I can't help thinking I was meant to reply.

I hope work is still keeping you on the level? Mine drives me mad sometimes but I wouldn't be without the contact with the children. They stop me from taking myself too seriously.

Take care,
Judith

Liz began to find some appeal in the idea that she could talk over her problems with someone not involved. Judith had shown a sensitivity and goodwill towards her situation, was non-judgemental and, above all, she didn't know any of them. Liz felt it would be a relief to talk about her problems. With someone interested and sympathetic she could open up in the knowledge that they would never meet. Judith could be a sounding board for her ideas and worries; for the things she found hard to say to Miles because he was part of the problem.

Anyway, she would take it gradually. Even a little light chatting back and forth couldn't hurt. She'd reply and just see how it went. Take it easy.

To: Judith Gower
From: Me

I don't actually live here, Judith. I'm staying in a friend's seaside bungalow. A few weeks ago my husband crashed his car into a tree. He'd been on the way to see this friend - we'd known him since our university days. Gareth never drank if he was driving but totally out of character, he seems to have drunk most of a bottle of whisky between leaving our house and hitting the tree an hour or so later. I think I now know what was going on in his mind. It's been nearly as bad as losing him, finding how much I didn't know about him.

Anyway, enough about me! What age group or subject do you teach? You mentioned your brother and being at the coast with him. I have no brothers or sisters. Actually that's probably why I'm launching into an email conversation with someone I don't know at all. I have nobody close. Gareth and I were, or I thought we were, a closed loop.
Thanks for thinking of me and writing back.

Liz

Miles came again for the weekend and they discussed her move. There hadn't been anything yet from the estate agent's except the usual proof copy of the leaflet about the house. He was checking every couple of days and forwarding the post to her, so she'd sent the copy back already, approved to go ahead. She really wanted a small property she could afford on her reduced income. There was some equity in the house and she had saved a little and would have life insurance money from Gareth but as her income was variable she didn't want to stretch herself too much.

On Saturday another message from Judith appeared in her inbox. She confessed to Miles that she'd had a reply and hadn't just deleted it.

"You daft girl. It could be anybody. You've heard about internet stalkers I suppose? You'll never get rid of him now!"

"He's a she for a start. I read it and replied. She wrote back again and now I'm going to read this and probably reply to it as well. She sounds okay and when I was at my lowest ebb, she held out a hand to me. That's how it felt, anyway."

Later, they had their little beach-combing session and, on their return, as she was getting to a crucial point in an illustration, Miles offered to do the dinner while she finished her task.

"Then you can email your stalker before we eat!" he said, laughing.

Liz completed her picture and set it aside to post on Monday. She always took digital photographs and emailed them off too. Then she had a good look at the latest email from Judith.

From: Judith Gower
To: Me

That's so sad about your husband. You implied you have an idea what was going on in his head. I will never ask but if you want to talk about it I will never tell, either.

I teach primary children, Liz. Top end of the school, just when they think they're practically teenagers (so naturally know everything!). Rob, my brother, teaches at a sixth form college. Teaching's a family thing – both our parents were teachers too. So I teach general subjects, as you do in a primary. He teaches, hell, what do they call it now? It's practical stuff. Woodwork, metalwork, probably now called Material Science or some such new name. He's handy to have around anyway!

I divorced my husband two years ago. He had gambled away our joint savings, we lost the house and I'll be in debt for years at this rate. I moved into Rob's spare room. Good thing we get on fairly well. I feel I need to give him his own space now so I'm looking for somewhere small to rent.

It's a shame you have no brother or sister to confide in. Rob was a godsend when I just wanted a moan or a rant. I'll be your honorary big sister if you like!

Take care, our kid. ;)
Jude

Liz wrote back straight away.

To: Judith Gower
From: Me

Hi Jude – I assume I can call you that now? It sounds like you've had a rotten time. It's like starting again straight out of university with all the debts and that. Rob sounds like a brother in a million.

Yes, I think I know what was bothering Gareth. I will probably tell you but not just this weekend. Our friend Miles is here – it's his place after all. He's been calling at my house and bringing or forwarding mail depending on how important he thinks it is.

I've decided to sell the house and get somewhere smaller. I'm not sure I could afford the mortgage on my own. As a freelance illustrator I only earn when the work comes in. Sometimes I'm flooded out but there are times when I've got nothing in the 'in-tray'.

Thanks again for listening.
Liz

8

The next two or three weeks passed in a flurry of small commissions, which kept the cash flow problem at bay, and messages from the estate agent who seemed convinced that the house would sell fairly quickly.

"I'm sure they say that to everyone, though," she said to Miles when he came one Sunday as usual.

"I never know how much of what they say is fact and how much is their usual sales patter. I had a look around, though. I went into their office and a couple of others just looking at similar houses and how much they're going for. Yours is priced pretty much in the middle of the range but it's on a big plot. That garden's going to be a selling point for lots of people. You've also got a new kitchen and bathroom and they'll help it to sell. It's not a place someone would feel they had to spend a lot of money on before they could move in. Things could start moving fairly quickly."

Liz put a casserole in the oven and they started out on their usual beach walk. They made their way for a couple of miles against the wind. The distances they covered never felt like the dry-land distance equivalents. Walking on sand was always much heavier going and the trudging steps sometimes made Liz's hips ache. They progressed at a slower pace too, because she insisted on inspecting the spreads of stones that lay in their path across the sand.

When they turned back, the weather began to worsen. A storm was coming in from the north. The sky blackened, bruised and lowered so that Liz felt she could reach up and touch the dark clouds just above her head. Thunder began to growl and, like a turned tap, the rain poured down, initially making big penny shapes in the sand, and finally thumping down and trickling down necks and between layers of clothing. The wind driving it chilled them to the core and their teeth chattered and their jaws ached trying to prevent it. It was the first time Liz had returned to the bungalow with barely a couple of stones instead of her usual handful.

They dashed indoors, she rushing for the bathroom while Miles stripped his sodden gear off in the bedroom.

"I'll get a quick shower to warm up," Liz said through clenched teeth, "then I'll make a hot drink while you get into the shower."

A grunt was the only reply she got, but within fifteen minutes they were both changed into warm dry clothing and clutching mugs of cocoa.

"That's the worst I've seen it while I've been here," Liz said, gradually beginning to thaw.

"It's worse in the winter," Miles said. "That's when the high tides can eat into the soft cliffs here and claw back the land. That's how the road disappeared. It used to turn and run parallel to the shoreline. It's the power of those waves that's responsible for smoothing that glass you're so fond of!"

They settled down to a plateful of steaming lamb hotpot each and a hush fell over the room, broken by the occasional sigh of satisfaction.

"There's nothing like a dousing in cold water followed by being flayed in a wind tunnel to give you an appetite," Miles said with a grin as he wiped his plate with a last bit of bread.

They washed up together in a companionable silence and then took a coffee each into the sitting room. It would take Miles a little under an hour to get home so they had most of the evening left.

"Heard anything more from your stalker?" he asked.

"Yes, and she is *not* my stalker!"

"Go on then. Why are you still in touch?"

"Oh, I suppose it's because, apart from you and Gareth, I kind of lost touch with friends after university. It's good to have someone uninvolved in my life that I can talk to. I used to throw myself into work, first for the agency and then even more fiercely when I was working on my own behalf and building up my client base. And, of course, Gareth and I seemed to feel that we didn't need anyone else. Oh! Sorry, sorry… Miles, I didn't mean… actually, he obviously did and I didn't know!"

"Liz, stop it. It doesn't matter now. The three of us made a good group, though there were two stronger bonds in there too."

"Yes, and now it's just us. Looking back with what I know now, it seems as though Gareth was the lynchpin. He was the one who related strongly to both of us. Without him we should have collapsed. Yet, although we'll never have that kind of relationship, I wouldn't be without your friendship, Miles."

"I wouldn't be without yours either. We're not just connected by his ghost, are we?"

They talked in a desultory manner about work and whether the storm would ease up, and eventually he decided to make a move.

"Look after yourself, Liz. If it helps chatting to your stalker…"

"Jude!"

"To Jude, then that's good. I know you and I have talked ourselves to a standstill these last few weeks but we're both so closely involved. Maybe an outside view helps?"

"Oh we don't usually talk about anything so serious! Of course, I had to tell her why I'd thrown the bottle in. It said on the message that I was a widow and I've told her about that, but we chat several times a week, just about trivia really. I tell her what I'm doing. I've even shown her some photos of what I've been working on. I know they won't go any further. She tells me about her kids at school and about her brother. She lodges with him at the moment. Long story and it's not really mine to tell."

"Never mind then. I won't ask. Just you be careful."

After he'd driven off she went to check her laptop again. As she'd expected, there was a message from Jude.

From: Judith Gower
To: Me

Hi Liz. I think I'm in with a bit of luck! I've found a flat to rent not too far from school (but far enough that I won't live next door to the kids I teach! That would put the tin hat on it). A friend of Rob's bought a house and has done it up and divided it into flats. I can have what he grandly calls 'The Garden Apartment' – or ground floor flat to the likes of us – for a sum I can manage each month. I'm going to have a look tomorrow evening after work. Keep your fingers crossed for me, girlie! I could be on the up and up!

Love,
Jude

Liz couldn't help the big daft grin that covered her face at this bit of good news. She hit 'Reply' straight away.

To: Judith Gower
From: Me

Great news, Jude! I hope it comes up to your expectations. It sounds a bit grand for you though. Will you have to get a whole new wardrobe of tea-gowns to wear there?

I said I'd probably tell you one day what I think tipped Gareth into drinking that whisky and hitting that tree. I hardly know how to start though. He, Miles and I had been close friends but it was only when I came here after his death and read a... shall I say, deeply affectionate dedication in a book he'd given Miles, that I realised the two of them had been lovers at uni, before I came along. I must sound like a daft tart but honestly, Jude, I had no idea – about either of them. Turns out I was Miles' rival but I didn't know. He must have hated me.

I think, well, I'm pretty certain, that Gareth and Miles were on the point of going back to their physical relationship again. Miles thinks Gareth drank the whisky so he would arrive at his house with no inhibitions. Then he'd have nothing stopping him from giving in to temptation. M doesn't think it was suicide, which was my first thought. I assumed he couldn't decide between us. I don't know what to think. If it was suicide I'm devastated to think he felt that bad. If it wasn't, I'm equally devastated to know he was going to resume an affair with Miles. With a bloke! What do you do? What do you think when that happens. And it's only because of the accident that it didn't happen.

Well, that's what my dilemma was/is. If he hadn't died, he might still not have been with me – though Miles thinks he would. He wanted children you see, which on my bad days makes me feel like rent-a-womb!

Well, there you have it. Sorry to burden you with all this. I'm starting to see my way out of it I think, though I still have huge self-doubt days. Miles is being a real friend. It probably sounds strange under the circumstances but we've always got on and we still do.

Thanks for being there.

Love,
Liz

She logged out, turned off the computer and went to bed. She knew Jude would reply as soon as she read the message but she didn't feel up to dealing with a reply after a long day. She'd look tomorrow.

9

There it was, next morning, when she opened her email.

From: Judith Gower
To: Me

Blimey kid! You don't half pick 'em! I could be glib and say how can you be married to someone and not really know them but I didn't know what I'd got myself into with Paul and the online gambling thing. I had no idea till the world fell in on me.

You do hear about people discovering love letters after their partner has died – but it's always a direct rival. A woman finds her husband had another woman – but to find he had a man! I can hardly imagine how it must have felt. You just can't pit yourself against that can you? Not that you had chance to but it could have come to that. You must have a very special friendship with Miles to overcome that sense of rivalry. Again, that probably wouldn't have happened if things had gone on the way you suspect they might. You would have been real rivals –

no holds barred, maybe?

All I can say is, no wonder you felt like lobbing that message out into the sea. It's like a cry to the whole universe. Stick with it girl. It's really not the end of your life and you've got to believe that. Good luck with the house-hunting – to both of us!

Love,
Jude x

Over the next few weeks, the estate agent phoned Liz on three occasions to let her know that someone was interested in the house. There were three visits and two couples went back a second time. It began to look like she'd have at least one offer in the near future. She kept Miles and Jude informed about the situation.

"If you accept an offer soon and want company when you look for somewhere to buy, you've only to let me know," Miles said. "I'm seriously nosy, you know!"

"Actually, that would be good if you're happy to do it. I'd feel a bit uncomfortable going someone's home on my own. I'd be glad of your advice too."

"On what?" he asked, crinkling a smile. "No cracks about gay men and their expertise in interior design if you don't mind!"

"Miles! I wouldn't dream!" She feigned shock at first, then they fell into uncontrolled laughter at the look on each other's face.

During those next few days, while Liz waited for one of the couples to come up with an offer, Jude proposed they should meet up.

From: Judith Gower
To: Me

Hi Liz. We're crossing the Humber Bridge on Friday night. Rob has an old college mate who we're catching up with. He lives near Hull and he's invited us to stay the weekend. I wondered how you'd feel if we popped over for an hour to see you in your little bungalow on Sunday afternoon, just before we go home? If you don't feel up to it for any reason, just say, okay? Only I know you usually have Miles there on a Sunday so you're not meeting two total strangers on your own.

Just let us know, either way. I feel we know each other fairly well now. It'll be like meeting an old friend - but different. You can show me where you chucked your bottle!

Cheers,
Jude x

Liz checked the diary - nothing to suggest Miles

wouldn't be there. She emailed straight back and said how much she was looking forward to seeing them. She would have been happy to meet Jude without Miles being there, though. She didn't know much about Rob except from bits of chat about him from Jude. Still, a friend's brother was welcome too. She knew Miles would insist on being there, even if he'd not intended to be. He was very protective of her and still had this 'stalker' worry.

She told him about the intended visit in an email on the Friday and said she was going to make a cake. Miles would understand the significance of that. Her last baking session was the prelude to her life's biggest disaster. He would know that if she could face a baking session, she was feeling good about the proposed meeting.

He arrived in the morning as he usually did and they made lunch together.

"Are we off for a walk or are you expecting Jude fairly early?"

"They're coming straight after lunch and Jude fancies a walk. She says Rob likes looking at beach pebbles. I've a feeling she wants to see the scene of my deepest embarrassment. Where I threw the bottle in!"

They'd just finished the washing-up after lunch when a car pulled up in the lane outside. Jude climbed out of the driver's seat. Liz had seen her picture - they'd exchanged photos with their emails -

but she hadn't expected her to be so dainty and petite. Rob climbed out of the passenger seat like a folding ruler, unfolding itself. He probably didn't top six feet by much, but next to his sister he looked immensely tall. The two made their way to the bungalow where Liz hurried to open the rarely used front door.

There was a rush of hugs from the girls, while Rob and Miles managed a polite handshake.

"Come in, have a drink!" Liz went into the kitchen to fill the kettle. "It's so great to meet you at last!"

"I know," Jude laughed. "People think I'm mad when I say one of my best friends is my MIAB girl - message in a bottle."

Liz breathed in sharply. "Oh, you haven't told everyone, have you?"

"Not what the message said. No, of course not. But I did say to people that I'd found a message in a green glass bottle. There's a sort of magic about the way it happened. Don't you reckon?"

Liz caught Miles' eye and she nodded.

"I think it was meant!" she agreed.

They sat chatting for half an hour and drank tea or coffee according to choice. Rob was a darling. Big and potentially clumsy, he was actually a gentle giant type, and was most definitely a classic 'What You See Is What You Get'. He had no side or pretence, just a straight forward manner and a good humour. Miles appeared withdrawn. This was possibly because he could hardly get a word in with the girls. He was in no way unfriendly but Liz felt like kicking him into gear to get him going.

"Come on then! Let's see the scene of the crime!" said Jude as she jumped up and went into the hall for her coat. The others followed her outside. They walked along the lane, line abreast, till they reached the low cliff and the muddy footholds down to the sand. At this point, Rob and Miles were walking side by side and fell to discussing the various specimens they stooped to pick up. After a brisk march they turned back and drew to a halt just before the muddy steps back up to the lane.

Liz stood with her back to the low cliffs and her hands in her pockets and looked out to the grey, crinkling water.

"This is the place," she said simply. "I ran down to the tide line with my bottle and hurled it as far as I could. I think I shouted something too… about my life being over. Then I fell on my knees in the breakers and sobbed."

Jude moved to her side and threw an arm round her shoulder.

They went back inside, all quiet now.

"It wasn't over, though," Miles said in a subdued tone. He sounded as if he felt the weight of his responsibility for her feelings of despair, although his relationship with Gareth had still been a secret at that point.

"No, of course it isn't," she agreed, and smiled to try to lift his mood.

Rob and Jude went into the kitchen to put the kettle on and leave them alone. Shortly afterwards she heard Rob commenting to Jude about the window-sill collection.

"Looks like you've got a broken bottle fetish!" he laughed, walking back into the sitting room with his hand full of green 'stones'.

"It does, doesn't it?" Liz agreed.

"I've got an idea for these," said Rob, waving a slack handful of her precious sea emeralds. "You really like them, don't you?"

"It's the colour really," Liz said. "It's so intense – I can't help picking them up, even though I know they are just something broken and worthless."

"I've got a tumble-polisher in the shed. It's something I used to do when I'd just graduated. I love bits of machinery and I love beach pebbles. It kind of linked them together. I could run these through the different grades of grit and polish them up for you."

"Oh, Rob! Would they really polish?"

"Oh yes, I'll say! I've seen various types of glass polished. Clear is lovely and the darker beer-bottle colour can come up like amber. It's worth a go. If you fancy it, that is?"

She fancied it alright! The idea that her dusty

looking bits of waste glass could end up looking like real jewels filled her with an unexpected joy.

"Here," she said, finding a polythene bag for them. "I'll just pack them up for you. How many can you do?"

"The lot if you like. From the look of things, it won't be long before you fill that glass again! I can easily send them back to you in a Jiffy bag. It'll take maybe 4 weeks?"

"That sounds fantastic, Rob. Thank you so much! Oh, I'm excited now!"

Jude gave a melodramatic sigh.

"When I said you have a lot to live for, I wasn't really thinking of broken bottles!" Rob laughed at them both. They took more tea into the living room and Liz happily cut into the first cake of her new life.

When they'd gone, Miles had to admit that Jude was an unlikely stalker and that Rob seemed a nice chap too.

"Considering that just about anybody could have picked up that message and got in touch, you've not done badly. It will be interesting to see how that glass turns out too!"

10

Jude told Liz in great excitement about her flat. She had been to see it and was enchanted. She couldn't get over the possibilities of the garden as an extra 'room' for entertaining and the compact flat was perfectly adequate for her needs. There was even a spare bedroom, although many would have termed it a box-room.

"How's your house-hunting going?" asked Jude. By now they had begun to phone one another occasionally, but usually their communications were still by email. The email wasn't as demanding as the insistent telephone. It was there when you were ready for it.

"Slowly," Liz admitted. "I've had three or four leaflets sent but there's not been one I think will do the trick. I feel I've been here long enough now, though, a bit like you did with Rob's spare bedroom, I expect."

"You need somewhere you can work in, don't you? It's not just a living space. It's your work area too. That's got to make it more critical."

"Well, there is one I thought might do. It's got a

fairly new loft conversion and there are two big Velux windows either side of the roof. It's going to be light up there but the rest of the house is jaded and tired. The loft's got a wooden staircase, according to the leaflet. An old bloke lived there till he went into a home recently. If he was frail, I don't suppose he ever went into the loft."

"Well, what's stopping you? That sounds like a perfect workroom for you. Not having to take down your stuff like you have to at the moment when Miles comes."

"I know. It's the thought of updating the rest of the house that's putting me off. It's not just decorating. It really needs a modern kitchen and a new bathroom. It's not even got a shower at the moment. I really don't want to be working in that situation with workmen all over the place. Nor do I want to sit here using up Miles' goodwill while the job is finished. Ideally I want a place I can walk straight into, but I don't have that kind of money to throw at it."

"I very much doubt he feels like that, Liz. Anyway, what have you got to lose by going to see it? I bet Rob would come and help you do it up at weekends. He's fantastically useful like that. He actually enjoys it – and you've no idea how much you can save by buying bathroom and kitchen units and doing the work yourself."

"Oh, I don't know, Jude. I'll have a word with

Miles. He's promised to come with me to check out any house I fancy."

"Go on then, flower. People don't say that to be polite. Get him to go with you and suss it out."

Liz rang the estate agent about the house she was interested in and arranged an early evening viewing in a couple of days' time. She then rang Miles who was not only happy to come with her, but seemed quite excited at the idea.

"I don't want to get my hopes up," she said, "because I gather it needs a lot doing to it. It's the potential for a permanent work room that's so tempting, though."

"Don't worry about doing the place up," Miles said. "I had to do loads to this flat and I really enjoyed the challenge. You feel it's yours in a special way when it's your own choice of kitchen and bathroom fitments. We'll have a recce to the showrooms this weekend if you decide you're going for it. It'll spur you on."

"Rob has offered to help me do the work as well," Liz told him. "Jude and he are excited about it too. It's mainly me that's doubtful."

Miles went quiet then and she found the phone call starting to peter out.

"Have you got a problem with Jude and Rob helping?" she asked, but Miles muttered something inaudible and cut the call short.

Liz wasn't sure what to make of Miles' sudden

strange attitude. Could he be jealous? When he felt that only he would be helping her, he was very positive and upbeat but as soon as she mentioned the others offering to help he shut down. Oh well, it was enough to cope with having to view the house without trying to keep on Miles' good side too.

On the day, they arrived at the property within minutes of one another and went to the door together. Liz had made the arrangement through the agent so it was perhaps unsurprising that they were greeted as 'Mr and Mrs Ellis'.

It was a member of the old gentleman's family who showed them around the house. Liz was pleased with the size and layout. True, the kitchen units were very basic painted wood and from the style they looked about fifty years old. The bath was ancient too, with green stains under the taps and there was nothing you could describe as a storage unit in the whole bathroom. The hand basin stood against the wall and the lavatory was a martyr to limescale. In front of the old man's son, they couldn't say much but Miles evidently felt as Liz did. She wouldn't want to move in and live here as it stood.

The two first-floor bedrooms, one at the front of the house and a smaller one sharing the back aspect with the bathroom, were a good size and in a reasonable decorative state. She could live with them, at least initially.

Ascending the uncarpeted wooden staircase to

the loft conversion felt like entering another world. Unlike the rooms downstairs, some mostly cleared, but still containing remnants of aged furniture which the son insisted would be removed before the sale, this room was completely empty. It was undecorated, having pine-clad walls which still retained the warm aroma of the wood. Liz knew she was staring, open-mouthed, at the large area in front of her. Miles was behind her, almost pushing to see in. She entered the room fully, twirled around, looked out of the angled windows and laughed a laugh of true pleasure. Despite the fact that they had agreed to play it cool in front of the vendor, she couldn't hold in her elation.

"Miles! This is so amazing!"

"It would certainly make a very good sized work area for you," he agreed. "It's going to need some units putting in. Maybe a long bench under that pair of windows." He indicated one side of the room.

"I could have movable easels there," she pointed as she spoke, "and my computer there." The ideas spilled out of them both.

"If you'd like to have a longer look around by yourselves," the son said, "I'll go back down to the kitchen and make a drink for us all. Would you like tea or coffee?" They both opted for a coffee and as he retreated down the stairs, Liz looked at Miles with the first genuine sparkle she'd had in her eyes since that dreadful Saturday.

"I love this room, Miles. Look, there are heaps of sockets. I could have a kettle there and save having to go down when I want a drink!"

"I know - I can see it in your eyes! What about the rest of the house, though?"

"That's the fly in the soup. Not sure I could cope with that ancient plumbing and the..." she checked the son wasn't coming back upstairs, "...grotty kitchen."

"That's where having practical friends will be handy," he said. "I'll be more than happy to come at weekends and work on the house if you decide to go for it. You can stay at the bungalow till you're happy with the state of this place."

She was so tempted.

"Let's go down for that coffee," she said with a smile.

***

During the next week, Liz accepted an offer on her place and confirmed her offer for the new house. She emailed Jude in a state of excitement.

To: Judith Gower
From: Me

I've had my offer accepted on that house with the loft conversion! The rest of the place is worse than tired. Loads of it needs ripping out and starting again but I can't let the chance of that home workspace slip away.

Miles is talking about working on it for me in evenings and weekends and I can stay at the bungalow till it's liveable! It's amazing, Jude. You'll love it - or you will when it's done!

Love
Liz x

11

After a flurry of solicitors' letters, phone calls and bank meetings, everything was eventually arranged for exchange of contracts and completion in a fortnight's time. Miles had organised surveyors and energy efficiency people as he held a key to Liz's house; he saved her hours in travelling time by doing so.

Her work schedule was picking up too and she really longed to get to grips with it in a new studio space. Jude had once again offered Rob as worker on the new house, but Liz felt a little unsure about approaching him. If he himself had offered, that would be different.

The day arrived when Liz was finally able to collect the keys. Her furniture had been put into storage and wouldn't be delivered to her new address until all the work and decoration was finished. She gave a set of keys to Miles and he took a day off work when the kitchen and bathroom fittings they had ordered were due for delivery.

Jude and Rob once again proposed a brief visit to see Liz in the bungalow. Again, they came on a

Sunday afternoon. Rob walked in with a huge smile on his face and held out a couple of glistening green gems which he dropped into her outstretched palm.

"Polish up a treat, your 'emeralds', don't they?"

"Oh! Wow!" Liz was astonished. "They are so stunning, Rob! They look deeper in colour and you can see right through them!" She held them out on her palm for Miles to admire. His face glowed briefly. She could tell he was impressed.

"I've still got the others. I'm working on an idea for them, if that's alright by you?" Rob looked a little anxious but then noticed that Liz had restocked the glass on the kitchen sill.

"Of course!" she said. "Take your time."

"Let me know when you're ready to get cracking on the new house," Rob said. "I've got a half-term week coming up. I reckon if I camp out at your new place I can get one of the big jobs completely out of the way. Kitchen or bathroom? You decide."

Miles looked distinctly put out at this.

"I've more or less put Miles in charge of operations, Rob. You'd better liaise with him. Thanks so much, though. That would really speed things up, wouldn't it?" she asked Miles. He nodded in agreement but still seemed a bit taciturn about it all.

Liz had to assume there was a degree of jealousy here. Miles didn't have the usual man to woman feelings for her but he was a solid, dependable friend and she loved him as you love anyone dear to you.

She didn't want him to feel hurt about this but neither did she want to tread on eggshells all the time in case he felt Rob was putting his nose out of joint. They made some sort of arrangement about doing the kitchen first and Liz agreed to Rob staying over in his half-term holiday. She really hoped this wasn't going to cause problems.

Jude, meanwhile, was bouncing around with the colour charts, fabric swatches and wallpaper samples Liz showed her.

"Oh, I know I'm so lucky having a newly decorated place to move into but I envy you being able to choose your own colours and stuff."

"I must admit, that's when it'll start to feel like mine," Liz said. She beamed like a lighthouse at the thought of bringing her artistic talents to the home she was creating.

***

Liz went to the new house on the day Rob was arriving for his week-long stint of camping out and home refurbishment. Miles would come along each evening and they'd work together. The plan was to ensure that the water was always switched on again each evening, whenever plumbing operations had required it to be off.

Rob turned up early, with a van stocked with an amazing array of woodworking and plumbing equipment. He brought a large circular saw and its bench right through the house to the patio at the back. The gardens were small, the front being essentially a parking area as the houses were terraced. The back consisted of the patio Rob intended to use as a work area, and a small lawn. He brought some of the equipment into the house and left some in the van till it was needed.

Liz stayed that first day and helped out in the role of labourer. She was pleased to see the progress the men were making. In the previous week, Miles had done a lot of ground work, stripping the 1970s wallpaper and taking out old units so they could start with a clean slate. She was enjoying both men's company, though she didn't think they were particularly enjoying one another's.

With Miles, her relationship was like putting on comfy shoes, awful as that might sound. They went back so far, had been friends for so long, that he required no effort from her. Rob, on the other hand, was a new friend. She knew so little about him other than that she was now close friends with his sister. Nevertheless, he treated life with a light touch and she enjoyed his company.

She couldn't fathom the source of Miles' antipathy towards Rob. He couldn't be jealous of her friendship with Rob. For one thing, it was new, tentative. She didn't know if it would go anywhere. She wasn't sure that she wanted it to. But Miles didn't want any other relationship with her than the one he already had.

Suddenly, Liz stopped. She felt a brick hit her brain. Did Miles fancy Rob? Was that what his unusually quiet, almost sulky, demeanour implied? Was it Liz herself he felt uncomfortable about when Rob was present? He always said there was a subtle body language he could pick up on. She knew she was as subtle as a poke in the eye with a stick. If anyone fancied her, they'd better tell her!

What a situation! She'd been enjoying Rob's company so much, relishing the interplay with another person, enjoying that it was a man. She didn't feel yet that it was the start of a relationship. Indeed, she didn't know if she was ready for one. But before it even became anything, were she and Miles destined to be rivals again?

She didn't know if Rob was gay. It was obvious he had no woman in his life at the moment but Jude had never mentioned whether he had ever had a girlfriend – or boyfriend. It just hadn't ever been part of their conversation and now it would look very pointed if she asked. She didn't want Jude to think she was interested in Rob in that way – especially if he really was gay. What a fool she'd look! After months of having her head stuffed with loneliness and grief, longing for male company, she now just wanted to run away back to the bungalow and shut the door on the world. Life could be such a bitch!

As the day wore on, Liz decided that whatever the situation was between the men, it was no business of hers. Rob continued to be jolly, chatty and friendly to both of them and Miles remained taciturn, gruff, not exactly unfriendly but certainly not as open as he usually was. Well, they could sort it out between themselves. All that mattered to Liz was that she got on with them both and, even better, they both got on with the job.

That aspect of the day seemed to be going very well indeed. Rob did the carpentry and Miles the plumbing, although he used a lot of Rob's tools. He was really set up to do this sort of job but no doubt that was because he taught practical subjects and had all his own equipment at home.

Liz fetched, carried, made tea and coffee and generally helped to keep things running smoothly. Eventually, after bringing in fish and chips for an evening meal, she decided she'd take herself back off to the bungalow for the evening.

"I could do with an early night now," she said. "I'm sure I shall discover new muscles when I wake up and find them aching!"

"I'll pack up soon too," Miles said. "The light's going and somehow it's never the same working in artificial light."

"Specially when it's as poor as this. I really must do some more shopping and get some spotlights for in here."

"I can put in low voltage lights and lower the ceiling a little, if you fancy?" Rob asked her.

"Now that does sound good. Maybe we need a shopping expedition together?"

"Shall I come too?" Miles sounded like a child left on his own in the playground.

"Of course! You know I've always admired your taste." At that comment, Liz and Miles exchanged a smile, remembering their conversation earlier.

They arranged to go the following evening. The superstore was open till ten at night and, as they weren't going to be working after about seven o'clock, they decided they'd meet Liz at a nearby pub and get a meal, then go and sort out some lighting for the kitchen.

"Might as well think of the other rooms too," she said. "I don't want to spend my life trailing around DIY stores!"

12

Liz returned to the bungalow after that first day with her mind in a racing turmoil. What the hell was going on? She was very close to Miles, and after his confession about Gareth, his honesty, she knew she always would be. But suppose Gareth hadn't died? Would she now still be grieving for her lost husband because he had moved in with Miles and left her? That would leave Miles definitely off her Christmas card list!

She could imagine how people felt when they had to face the world and tell all their friends that their husband had run off with another woman. How would you tell them that he'd preferred a man over you? How would that have knocked, no, massacred, her self-confidence? She realised that she was re-evaluating her friendship with Miles in the light of this knowledge – the knowledge that she and he seemed to like the same men.

It was too early, and her grief for Gareth was too raw, for her to be seriously thinking about another relationship. She really did still grieve for her dead husband, even though she knew that he might have been unfaithful to her by now, had he not died. She loved him; she still missed him. Even so, she felt herself being drawn to what she saw as Rob's uncomplicated, outgoing nature. She was an acquaintance, a friend of his sister's. She knew she would like to be his friend too. Would she like to be more? She didn't know – but she definitely wanted that door left open.

How would she view Miles if he and Rob formed the relationship that she suspected? It was going to strain a close friendship she had come to rely on. Her thoughts tumbled around that evening and she found herself thinking of a glass or two of wine to clear them – maybe to turn them to another topic. This one was done to death; she could find no solution in thinking and worrying but she couldn't drop it. She couldn't stop fearing that Miles would steal another man from her. Except that it was the other way round before, wasn't it? Last time, she had stolen his.

She opened a bottle of red and her laptop. She'd better let Jude know how the day's work on the house had gone.

To: *Judith Gower*
From: *Me*

Evening Jude. I think we're already making progress on the house. Your brother is amazing! He turned up like a proper chippy with all his gear and saws and stuff and he was off. Miles had already got the kitchen and bathroom stripped of the old stuff, carpeting included, so we were off to a flying start. When I left this evening there was a new sink and mixer taps installed by Miles and the first of the base units put in by Rob. Each does his own job and they crack on.

Tomorrow evening I'm going back over and we're going to grab a pub meal then go and buy light fittings at a big DIY place. The old bulbs in there are pretty crummy but to be honest, I think after a day's work the lads could do with the evening off, light or no light.

I really like your brother. He's so open and friendly and after all the grief and angst, he's a breath of fresh air.

I'll keep you up to date with progress. Thanks for suggesting this job to him.

Love,
Liz x

That was about as far as she dared go about her feelings for Rob. They were just tender shoots at the moment anyway, but she would have liked to know if she was wasting her time. Should she be getting ready to congratulate Miles on his new relationship? Oh, it was hopeless to speculate. She finished her wine and went to bed, exhausted enough by the day to fall into a deep sleep.

Next morning she found an email from Jude.

From: Judith Gower
To: Me

Hey sweetie! So glad your lads are making progress. I'm really enjoying this half term week as it's giving me a chance to get used to my new surroundings. I'm so enjoying the garden – going out there to sit and read, or taking a hot drink out.

Send me some pics, will you? I've sort of seen the 'befores' from the estate agent's leaflet – a bit grim, I must say, but so much scope. Let me see some 'afters' when you've got it done – or even 'part ways' will be good.

Take care,
Jude x

So, no answer there then, but to be fair, she hadn't asked a question. Not directly. With a big sigh, Liz filled the kettle and made a drink to go with her breakfast.

She had a text message from Miles later that morning and it was accompanied by a photograph. Already the kitchen looked amazing. Miles had skimmed the walls because stripping the ancient and horrible wallpaper had removed some of the plaster too and the surface was trashed. Now, the new units, the sink, the clean lines of the smooth walls made it look like a magazine illustration. Miles said they still had to put the cooker in but were waiting for the new lights so they could do all the electrics together. She sent a reply saying how pleased she was, and that she was looking forward to meeting them tonight.

She called a halt to the job she was finishing and decided to take a walk along the beach again. Not only the fresh air, but the mental abstraction of checking over the patches of stones with the top layer of her mind would help to clear her frustration and anxiety. Just having that to take her attention away from her own problems was a godsend.

Right, she thought. Let's assume that Miles and Rob will end up as an item. If that's the worst that could happen, it's not too bad. She had no prior claim on Rob, no real deep knowledge of him yet. Certainly not the kind of knowledge of another person that you had to have if you were to form a deep relationship. Yet she realised that in spending time working together, the two men had that opportunity to develop a friendship – or more. She was on the periphery here, not involved with either. Rob was a friend; Miles was a friend. Where's the problem?

With another few stones in her pocket she went

back into the bungalow and added them to her windowsill collection. She paused to pick up the two polished glass pieces that Rob had dropped into her palm recently. He had a plan for the others. Whatever could he have meant by that? She found herself rubbing the smooth, rounded glass nuggets between finger and thumb. Somehow, the action was soothing, calming. Almost without thinking, she put one of the shiny, sea-glass gems into her pocket and continued to fondle and smooth it with her fingers as she went through to finish her piece of work.

She made a small sandwich for a late lunch, not wanting to take the edge off a pub dinner, but too hungry to wait. When the time came to get ready for the journey, she picked up her camera and added it to her big holdall, and made sure she had her credit card. It was looking like Big Spend Day at the DIY store.

She set off in the car with her heart a little lighter than it had been of late. She tried to sit on her feelings. She knew she was looking forward to seeing Miles again, but largely, to spending a little more time with Rob. If she didn't, how would she ever get to know him? How would she find out if he could really be a friend, or even more than a friend?

Liz went straight to the house and let herself in. She wandered slowly through to the kitchen, listening out for the voices. She could hear Rob chatting and singing along to music from the radio.

Not much more than the occasional mumble seemed to be coming from Miles, though. Mind you, he was always quiet when he was working, concentrating. She walked into the room and all but the radio fell silent.

"Wow!" That was all she could say. "Just wow! You're making a brilliant job of it!"

For the moment, did they look shifty? There was a silence she couldn't account for, then both tried to talk at once.

"You can really see the progress we've made today," from Miles.

"I'm so glad you're pleased," from Rob.

"Of course I'm pleased!" she said. "It looks like a different room. You've changed the whole look of it already. Once you're finished and the walls are painted and the curtains are up… I don't know what to say except thank you both so much!"

Instinctively, she gave Miles a hug. It's what she would always have done in the circumstances. Then, turning to Rob, she faltered. Would he think she was being a bit forward, as her mother would say? Oh, to hell with it. She threw her arms around the very sheepish looking man, covered as he was with fragrant sawdust, and gave him a squeeze. To her surprise, after a fraction of a second, he squeezed her in return.

She pulled away and looked at them both. Miles gave her his usual lazy smile, and a ghost of a wink.

Rob looked cute in pink. Blushing suited him!

"Come on," she said, wondering where to look and finding herself possibly the most embarrassed of the three. "I'm starving! Are you at a convenient stage to stop? I'll take a few pictures first – Jude's demanding them! Then, dinner's my treat – it's the least I can do."

After they ate, they went to the DIY store to check out the lighting. She chose a cluster of fancy lights for the living room, elegant and looking like calla lilies in shape, with frosted glass shades. She also bought a standard lamp with the same small bulbs and lily-like shades. It was the first time she'd chosen entirely by herself. When she and Gareth had decorated their home, it had, she realised, always been a compromise. She could ask the men their opinions, see what they thought about the suitability of her choice, but it was definitely her place to make that choice. The kitchen lights were fairly straight forward. It was just a matter of deciding how many she'd need, in an even spread across the ceiling. Rob ordered the board that he'd need to drop the ceiling by a few inches.

"Right, we're off!" he said. "It's not going to take too long to do that job. It's going to make the room look much better with an even light too. You always seem to cast a shadow on your work-surface with a central kitchen light."

"Not much of a shadow with a 100-watt bulb,

though," said Miles.

"Haha! Have you thought about a couple of small strip lights above your work-surfaces Liz?" asked Rob "Easy enough to fit while I'm doing the electrics."

"I hadn't actually. We had them at home…" She faltered. Suddenly, what she was doing hit her like a smack in the face. She was starting afresh without Gareth. Of course she was – she *knew* she was – but she had tried not to advert to it, even to herself.

"We had them at the old house," she continued, "but I'd forgotten to add them to my shopping list. Yes. Let's go for it. I don't know how to thank you both for all this."

She noticed a smile pass between them. Just a glance, a twitch of the lips – almost a secret smile. Hell. She'd been right. There was definitely something going on between them. Well, good luck to them, she thought. Miles deserved some happiness.

They took the purchases back to the house and there she discovered that Miles had ripped up the carpets in the living room and bedrooms. They were very old-fashioned in design and were worn and even sticky in places. Heaven knew what had been spilt on them over the years.

"These boards aren't bad," Rob said. "They're the old-fashioned wide floor-boards. Seems a shame to cover them up."

"Oh, they're gorgeous!" Liz loved real wood and they appealed to her a great deal more than some cheap carpet. "Maybe I'll get them sanded and waxed eventually. Well, it'll save me a fortune in underlay and carpet if I do."

"I think once we've got the bathroom done too – should have them both finished by weekend – you can move in if you like," said Rob. "There'll still be the decorating of the other rooms – I'm happy to pop along at weekends and help with that of course. But the two worst rooms of the house will be up to standard."

"Oh, I'd love to move as soon as possible! Oh, Miles, I don't mean that to sound ungrateful. I hope you know you've been a lifesaver in letting me use the bungalow. I couldn't have gone back to the home I'd shared with Gareth. But there's nothing like your own front door – and of course, you can have full use of your sea-side bungalow back."

"Don't worry, Liz. I know you're grateful and I agree. This is the fresh start you need." Again, there was that little glance between Miles and Rob. A secret shared. She was excluded. Oh well. If that's the way it was, fair enough. They were entitled to their own happiness and there was no doubt that they were both working flat out to try to make her happy.

Liz looked forward to moving into the house at the end of the following week. Rob would be back at work on the Monday but Miles said he'd continue to finish up bits and pieces straight from work for the rest of the week. He rang a removal company and arranged for them to collect Liz's furniture from storage and deliver it on the Saturday. She'd have all her own things around her and her own home, albeit in need of decoration. At least most of the old ghastly wallpaper had gone. Miles was thorough!

At the end of the half-term week, she and Jude called at the house. It was to be Jude's first real view of the place, though she'd been keeping up with the job through the photos Liz had sent her. She said she could already see how fantastic it would be with Liz's choice of soft furnishings and paint. Liz had measured up and ordered curtains in her chosen fabrics but knew it would be some time before she'd get around to painting the woodwork and the newly-skimmed plaster of the walls.

Once again, she knew she wasn't imagining it when she went into the house, heard chatter and noticed it die away, felt the frost fall as she entered the bathroom where they were working. Just for an instant, they looked guilty as if caught out at something and surely she didn't imagine the look that passed between them before they both set eyes on Jude, who came in behind her.

"Hey! Great to see you!" said Rob. "How are we doing?"

"It's amazing! You're quite a team, aren't they,

Liz?"

"Certainly are," she admitted. Blimey, it wasn't just her imagination then. Jude could sense something going on between the men.

"Just finishing up here," said Miles. "Rob can start packing the van while I clear up."

"Great stuff. I've rather enjoyed camping out. Reminds me of my younger days!" Rob began carting his belongings into the van where most of the equipment had already been stowed.

"Can we all come again next Saturday?" asked Jude. "It would be lovely to be here when you move into your new home at last."

"Of course you can!" Liz hadn't even thought of it. "I'd love to see you, any time. You can help me unpack the stuff. Boxes of clothes and kitchen equipment - it'd take an age to do it myself. I'll press you into service if you come!"

"Well, I'm happy to help," Rob said, once again glancing at Miles before giving his sister a grin.

They went their separate ways that evening with the arrangement that they'd meet here again at nine the following Saturday.

"I can hardly wait!" said Jude. "You must be beside yourself?"

"I'm certainly more excited about it than I thought I'd be," Liz admitted. "Initially a new place was an escape from the ruins of my old life."

Miles put his hand in the small of her back. It

was such a tiny gesture but it said so much.

13

Liz was determined to let it all go for the next week. Anything to do with the house was out of her hands now. She tried not to think about the developing relationship between Miles and Rob either. Like the relationship between Miles and Gareth, it was also out of her hands and she could do nothing to affect it. In fact, as she kept telling herself, if Rob had made a move with her, would she have accepted it or was it too soon? How long had she been a widow? Four months? If anyone had told her of this happening to someone else she'd have called it unseemly haste.

Yet she knew she didn't want an affair, didn't want a new man in her life – not yet, anyway. No. What really kept all this grinding about in her brain was that she had a new friend, Rob. He was evidently a good friend – who would spend a whole week of his holiday doing up someone else's house otherwise? Yet always, in her mind's basement, was the rumbling thought that he might be doing it to be with Miles. Maybe it had nothing at all to do with her. How could she find out from Jude if Rob was gay without asking it? She couldn't! She settled in front of her laptop for a few minutes anyway, just to chat.

To: Judith Gower
From: Me

Hi Jude! I'm on tenterhooks now while I wait till Saturday to see how it all turns out. I know I've still got a lot to do to the place but the bulk of it, the bit that put me off buying, is done with! I'm so glad you're all going to be there with me on the day when it comes to moving in. I keep thinking about how I felt back then when I lobbed that bottle into the sea. I thought that was it for me. I didn't think I'd ever be happy, look forward to, or enjoy anything ever again. I can't believe how wrong I was.

I don't mean I've got over my husband's death. There's a way in which I never will. I'll accept that it's in my past and that there's more than I ever thought in my future. The best thing about all this was that you found the message and replied. How lucky was I in that? And now Rob. All the work he's doing. I must ask, did you ask him to or was it his own idea? I'd hate to think he's used his holiday up because big sister had twisted his arm! Anyway, he's a find and no mistake – and all because of that message in a bottle. Fairy tales do come true!

Liz x

No. She couldn't ask Jude. Then it occurred to her that maybe, tentatively, she could broach it with Miles. Not outright, of course. It would be rude; intrusive and insensitive. But she could chat, couldn't she? While she had the laptop switched on, she began an email to him. She had a question she wanted him to answer.

To: Miles Jeffries
From: Me

Hi, Miles. I can't believe how good the place is looking. You and Rob have worked absolute wonders. You seem to be getting on ok now? Initially I feared you wouldn't. You seemed a bit quiet when he was around – maybe it's just having a stranger foisted on you? Anyway, I'm really looking forward to getting moved in. I'll take the rest of the jobs steadily – the painting and such.

By the way, the shop told me the curtains are ready to collect. If you have a minute, would you mind picking them up for me? They're all paid for. Then we can get them hung on Saturday too. Whooo – exciting times. I never thought I'd be excited again. Just goes to show.

Thanks for all the work you've done. You can't have had an evening to yourself last week. I wondered about asking you all to stay on Saturday night? There'll be a couple of beds and the sofa-bed too. We can work out who'll go where later. Then I could get some pizzas in and a couple of bottles of wine and we can celebrate my new start together. What do you think?

Love,
Liz x

She switched off the computer and went back to work. It was an interesting commission and one she was enjoying so she immersed herself in it to the extent that she was surprised to find she'd missed her usual lunch-time. She decided to have an early dinner and work in the evening.

She was thinking of her new work area in the house in town. The men had been so busy with the kitchen and bathroom but she was sure she could pick up an old dining table for a short term fix and use that as a work bench. There'd still be loads more space than there was here.

***

The rest of the week passed like a watched pot - it dragged in spite of regular emails from Miles and Jude. Neither of them even mentioned Rob in their messages. Had it all been in her imagination, then? Both of them replied to her, but in a sentence or two. They both led busy lives and she had to remind herself that she might be lonely here in her seaside outpost, but others were out at work, stuck with fixed timetables, and weren't hanging about waiting for her every word. Miles had replied to say that it sounded like an excellent idea that the four of them, all so involved in the new house, should 'christen' it on Saturday evening. Jude liked the idea of staying on Saturday too and said she'd mention it to Rob.

On Friday Liz decided she'd better think about packing her things. She didn't have much with her. She'd brought a couple of cases of clothes, the second lot when she'd realised she would never go back to live in the old home. Her work materials were also here and she reached a stage in her current project where she could stop and begin sorting and packing those in boxes. She stopped for a break and decided to take a last walk along the shore.

The recent weather had been stormy so she'd not been out for a few days. The beach looked different today. Instead of tongues of pebbles licking up from the water's edge to the high tide line, the pebbles were spread along the beach parallel to the sea's edge. Close by the water, where she usually found many of the smaller pebbles, the surface of the 'pebble slick' was sprinkled with sand and sea-weed, tossed up in the storm. It wasn't so easy to see the individual stones.

She walked higher up the beach and eventually found a few interesting things to add to her collection. She wondered what she'd do with them all now. She'd have to pack them in a box or a polythene bag and take them with her. Perhaps they could go on her new kitchen windowsill as a reminder of her beach-combing days. She thought of the things she'd found on this beach. Not only stones and glass. She'd found the courage to go on with her life and some new friends who, touched by her despair, had reached out to her and were happy to share in that new start. Putting her hand in her trouser pocket for a tissue, she found one of the polished glass fragments Rob had given her a few weeks previously. She rubbed it again and absorbed the comfort it offered.

Back at the bungalow, she prepared her last meal there, apart from tomorrow's cereal. Afterwards, she packed her gear into the car. She wanted an early start. There was lots to do in the morning and they were meeting at nine. Finally, she ended the day as she'd ended so many while she'd stayed there – browsing Miles' bookshelves. She looked at the fateful War Poets book that had tipped her off to her husband's relationship with his friend. Would things have been any different if she'd never known? Her mood had become a little melancholy and the poems suited it. She read till her eyes were gritty with tiredness, then she took a fresh cup of tea to bed.

14

Liz arrived at her new address with her belongings in the car boot and her hopes up in the air. Rob's van was already there, with Jude as a passenger, and she'd barely got out of her own vehicle when Miles walked up and met them at the door. She unlocked it in a ceremonious manner – Miles had a key too so it wasn't necessary for her to do it but it felt important. Portentous.

The first thing she noticed when she went in was the smell. Paint. She looked into the living room and, yes! Her chosen colour was on the walls and one of them - it must have been Miles because Rob had been back home in Lincolnshire all week - had sanded and waxed the floorboards to a warm honeyed sheen.

"Oh! Oh look at this! I don't know what to say!" They were all watching her closely.

"And the curtains! You've hung the curtains too – oh Miles! You're an absolute star!"

She stepped into the echoing living room and, throwing her arms wide, she twirled around to take it all in.

"It's fabulous!"

"It wasn't all me, you know," Miles confessed. "These two have been pretty busy this week too. Rob came over straight after school twice. While I did the floors, he got on with the workroom. They were late nights but, hey, we enjoyed ourselves!" He and Rob clapped each other on the shoulder and exchanged big grins.

"The workroom?" She rushed up the stairs and they all followed, faces breaking into wide smiles. Rob had put in the long workbench they'd talked about, with drawer units and cupboards beneath to store her materials. Along the opposite wall was a small sink with a worktop, socket and kettle. It was all here – all the things she'd talked of.

"Oh, you've all been so good," she said, on the verge of crying.

"Is that the van?" Jude linked arms with her and they went back down the stairs to open the door, while she pulled herself together.

The day went so fast. As they directed the men from the storage firm who took all the furniture to the correct rooms, she saw that the bedrooms too had been painted and their floors sanded. It was so perfect. After the van men had left, the four of them put beds together, made them up with bedding and unpacked clothing, which she and Jude proceeded to sort into the wardrobe. There were no fitted ones here but she had a large one from her previous life, as she was beginning to think of it, which had come with the other furniture.

She postitioned her bookshelves and added books and the place really looked like a home. She flopped onto the sofa with a satisfied smile as Miles said he'd make tea and coffee for them all. Jude disappeared into Rob's van for a few seconds and came back with a couple of black bin-bags.

"What's this?" Liz asked, as Jude dumped them in front of her.

"Have a look!"

She tipped out the contents – two large cushions per bin-bag, and covered in the very same fabric she'd chosen for the curtains.

"Jude! How did you manage this?"

"I sneaked a pic of your samples with my camera-phone. Ordered the stuff off the internet and that's why I've been a bit preoccupied all week!"

"You made them? You made me cushions to go with..." Liz spread her arms to indicate the whole of the living room and then she could contain herself no longer. She cried, huge, happy, heart-filled sobs of joy.

"Oh, you wonderful lot! I can't thank you enough for all this. I really can't. And I know I keep repeating myself but... thank you!"

"Come on, dry up or your eyes'll go all puffy," said the ever-practical Jude. "Let's go and get those pizzas. I'll buy the wine!"

Later that evening, when the bottles were empty, the pizzas nothing but crumbs and they were all clutching mugs of coffee, Liz insisted on hearing all about the subterfuge that had gone on behind her back.

"I admit that initially I thought Rob had... erm... designs on you," Miles said, sounding a bit prissy.

"Me? Designs?" Rob tried for a look of total innocence.

"Haha! You were being protective then?" Liz was cheered to think that Miles was looking out for her.

"Yep," Miles said. "I'm your minder!"

Liz laughed, both at the idea that she needed a minder, and at the way she'd so badly misinterpreted his thoughts and intentions toward Rob.

"Rob knows about me," he said. "We had a lot of time to talk, while we were working here. He knew about Gareth's death in the crash, from Jude. He didn't know about me and Gareth, though, but I told him. It's been a relief to talk about it with someone not involved. I think that's what you said about your 'stalker' earlier?" He indicated Jude with his eyes and Liz nodded.

"Me? Your stalker?" Jude erupted with laughter. "Cheeky beggars!"

"So I've been thinking you and Rob had a thing going! The way you stopped talking when I came into the room, or exchanged little glances – I honestly thought…"

"You thought I was gay!" Rob pointed at his chest and laughed.

"You thought I fancied the same bloke as you – again!" When Miles said this, Liz blushed furiously.

"Well, you do, just a bit, don't you?" Jude asked.

"Oh, leave the poor lass alone!" Rob said, which almost made her feel worse.

"I don't know what I feel. I love all of you with a 'special friends' kind of love. I don't know what else to say, really. It's just too soon…"

"Of course it is," said Jude. "Now behave yourselves, you two!"

"There were times we'd been discussing me coming back over straight from school so I could do your workroom, and when you came in, we wondered if you'd heard anything – how long you'd been there and if we'd given the game away. That's why we stopped talking when you appeared suddenly," Rob said.

"And no doubt we looked as shifty as hell," Miles said. "It was all about surprising you, though. We wanted to get the paint, finish the rooms, sand the floors. There was a lot being planned on the quiet!"

They were all exhausted and ready for bed when Liz asked who would sleep where.

"Shall Rob and I share then?" asked Miles,

stifling a laugh.

"Please yourselves," she replied, and laughed with him. In the event, Rob had his sleeping bag in the van. He slipped out for it.

"Rob does like you, though," said Jude.

"It's mutual," Liz replied, "but it's just too soon. Far too soon."

"Of course it is, sweetie. Just remember it's there, though."

Rob returned with his bed-roll and a small, rather messily wrapped, package in his hands. He tossed it to Liz, who fumbled with it and almost dropped it.

"What's this?"

"Why do people always say that?" Miles asked. "Have a look! We're all as nosy as you!" She opened the little packet and out dropped a string of beads. It was her sea-glass nuggets, drilled through and linked with silver wire to make a beautiful necklace. It was just so gorgeous.

"Rob! Have you made this?"

"Yes. If you break a bottle, you can't remake the bottle. You can make something else with it, though. Maybe something even better."

The End

Thanks

I would like to thank the following friends.

Andy Barrett – thanks for your insightful comments on an earlier draft.

Thanks to Cornelius Harker and my closest male relative by marriage, Richard Middleton, for reading the story and telling me if it works.

And thank you to Jonathan Hill, editor, cover-designer and publisher, without whom there'd be no *Message in a Bottle*.

Contact

www.kathmiddletonbooks.com

www.facebook.com/ignite.bookblog

www.twitter.com/kathmidd

Also Available

RAVENFOLD

A novella by Kath Middleton

Fourteen year old Romelda Bolt lives at a time when a woman is a man's property. Her parents, promised wealth by a local lord three times her age, marry her off. A brutal and bullying relationship is born.

Romelda's life will change the course of history in her village. Can she and her pet raven change the family's future too?

"Had I not been aware that this is the author's first story other than drabbles, I would have thought the book was written by a much more experienced writer. The dialogue and narrative are true to the era and the storyline flows seamlessly." - *Jennifer Hanning, Author*

"An unusual and gripping historical novel; highly recommended." - *Cathy, Indie Bookworm*

Also Available

BEYOND 100 DRABBLES

Flash fiction by Jonathan Hill and Kath Middleton

'Beyond 100 Drabbles' features 120 new miniature works, written by two of today's most formidable drabblers. Jonathan Hill and Kath Middleton showcase some of their finest drabbles here, resulting in a collection that demonstrates the indisputable power of this popular flash fiction form.

The authors cover a plethora of genres and even take the drabble one step further by interacting in a series of 'challenge drabbles'.

"Addictive!" - *Nicola Palmer, Author*

"Brilliant variety of little gems." - *Sujay, Amazon reviewer*

"It's great to see the form receiving quality releases like this... highly recommended." - *Michael Brookes, Author*

Made in the USA
Charleston, SC
15 August 2014